Call Me Mimi

FRANCIS CHALIFOUR

TUNDRA BOOKS

Published in Canada by Tundra Books,
75 Sherbourne Street, Toronto, Ontario M5A 2P9

Published in the United States by Tundra Books of Northern New York,
P.O. Box 1030, Plattsburgh, New York 12901

Library of Congress Control Number: 2007927391

Library and Archives Canada Cataloguing in Publication

Chalifour, Francis
    Call me Mimi / Francis Chalifour.

ISBN 978-0-88776-823-1

    I. Title.

PS8555.H2758C36 2008   jC813'.6   C2007-902729-6

We acknowledge the financial support of the Government of Canada
through the Book Publishing Industry Development Program (BPIDP)
and that of the Government of Ontario through the Ontario Media
Development Corporation's Ontario Book Initiative. We further
acknowledge the support of the Canada Council for the Arts and the
Ontario Arts Council for our publishing program.   ONTARIO ARTS COUNCIL
                                                     CONSEIL DES ARTS DE L'ONTARIO

Design: Leah Springate

Typeset in Mrs. Eaves

This book is printed on acid-free paper that is 100% recycled,
ancient-forest friendly (40% post-consumer recycled).

Printed and bound in Canada

1   2   3   4   5   6   13   12   11   10   09   08

To those who have been bullied

Acknowledgments

Thanks to all my students from grades one to ten: You were great sources of inspiration throughout my career as a teacher! Thanks to my colleagues at École secondaire Étienne-Brûlé in Toronto as well as at the Literacy and Numeracy Secretariat of the Ontario Ministry of Education, where enthusiasm for learning is always nurtured.

Thanks to my friend and agent, Michael Levine, and my editor, Kathy Lowinger.

J'aimerais remercier ma famille pour leur appui constant: Maman, Mario, Tante Yvonne, Sylvie, Réal, France, et Daniel.

Thanks to my professors at the University of Ottawa and the University of Toronto: Kristen Vanstone, for your course on astronomy, and Dr. Claire Duchesne.

Thanks to the staff of the Robarts Library at the University of Toronto for your assistance with my research on bullying and self-esteem.

Thanks to my friends: Luc Bernard, Chantal Carrier, Isabelle Carrier, Lily Dabby, Lisette Falker, Charles Gibbs, Jacques Goulet, Allen Kwong, Joe Labao, Michelle Marcelin, Jamie McKnight, Lionel Pardin, Mark Prior, Seamus O'Reagan, Sharon Silver, and Craig Zadan. As for those who don't find their names on this brief list, please call me so I can invite you for dinner.

"Courage is doing what you are afraid to do.
There can be no courage unless you're scared."
— EDDIE RICKENBACKER (1890–1973)

Chapter One

*C*all me Mimi. I used to be a pretty normal kid (I think) until high school, when I was accepted at St. Mary's Academy for Girls. It was supposed to be my path to a golden future, but instead, I got lost. My body ballooned while I sort of shriveled up inside. There's a fine line between what's real and what isn't, between being real and being a stranger in your own skin. This is the story of how I found myself again. It may not seem like a big deal to you, but for me, it's been like Columbus discovering a whole new continent. It's not always a picnic, being real. But now that I've tried both, I'll pick real anytime.

♡

Nobody knew about even one of my secret lives except for Patricia Tahir. She was a transfer student, the only person at St. Mary's Academy for Girls who liked me, and she was certainly the only person who was bigger than me. Everybody tormented me about my size. Nobody tormented Patricia. Nobody dared. Legend had it that, back in Cameroon, she'd killed a lion with nothing but her manicured hands. I knew this couldn't be true because she'd grown up in Paris, in a family of diplomats. But the legend stuck.

I was hunched over my notebook at a remote table in the cafeteria when I sensed Patricia standing over me with her tray. "What are you doing, Mimi?" She looked over my shoulder. "It looks like you're writing a speech. An acceptance speech. What's it for?"

While she arranged her plate of shepherd's pie, her glass of milk, her butter tarts, and her nod to good health – an apple – on the table and propped the tray against her chair, I debated: If she found out what I was doing, I would make my only friend in the school think I was nuts. On the other hand, there was the tempting possibility of relief in telling somebody. Something about Patricia was so supremely unflappable that before I could stop myself, I blurted it out.

"It's in case I ever win a beauty pageant."

I braced myself for her big boom of a laugh. It didn't come. All she said was "It's good to be prepared, I guess," and set about methodically eating her lunch.

Mimi, the Beauty Queen was only one of my secret lives. I had several, all featuring a wise and bright, self-confident and lovely Mimi.

Mimi, the Beauty Queen

I am taking the laundry to Monique at the Laundromat when a big, apple red car drives up beside me. The smoked window opens and the lady in the backseat calls me over. She hands me her telephone number on a pink Post-it, with a rose in the corner, and begs me to be in the beauty pageant she is organizing. I am reluctant. After all, I am a straight A student (that part was true – also fat and homely, but that doesn't play a role in the fantasy) *and above such superficiality. She is persistent. Think of how much good I could do as an example to more frivolous teenagers. I finally agree to enter the pageant on the condition that I can donate all my winnings to orphans. Thus I would have it all: acclaim for my looks and the superior feeling of knowing that my looks don't count, all at once.*

♡

Patricia was fascinated. She never told anyone (believe me, I would have heard about it if she had), although every now and then she'd ask me what I was planning to wear in the, say, evening-gown category. Then she moved to Ottawa and I was on my own again.

There were other fantasies I kept to myself.

Mimi, the Queen's Confidante

Queen Elizabeth comes to our school. Macy Moore is chosen to show her around because her family is, after all, Montréal royalty. Queen Elizabeth listens to Macy prattle on for a moment or two and then says, "Enough of this! I want a girl with substance, with poise and grace, to show me around St. Mary's. And that girl is Mimi Morissette!" We soon become close friends. She confides in me about the problems she has with her children and I offer my wise counsel. She invites me to live in Buckingham Palace so that I can give sage advice whenever needed. She gives me a corgi.

Then there was the Céline Dion fantasy.

Mimi, Friend of the Stars

Céline is driving along our street in the back of her limou-sine. I am pushing Mrs. Jaeger's wheelchair (Mrs. Jaeger lives across the hall and is both sweet and quite capable of pushing her own wheelchair). Céline sees me and rolls down her window. "You seem like a kind person. I need an unbiased opinion. Which of these rings do you like best?" She holds her jewel-bedecked hand out to me and two emeralds flash. "I think that natural is best. You don't need rings," I answer. "Someone who is honest! You must become my special companion, thanks to your down-to-earth sincerity!" I modestly demur. After all,

Maman would worry about my living a star's life. "Never mind. I appreciate family too," Céline reassures me. "Both of you can live in my mansion in Las Vegas."

♡

But the fantasy that I loved best was the most far-fetched of all. It was about my father.

Mimi, the Daughter

I fumble with the key to our apartment because the bitter, wintry walk from school has numbed my fingers. A warm gust of candle-scented air greets me as I open the front door. I hear the comforting order of a Bach fugue coming from the radio. My father calls out from the leather armchair, "Mimi, my darling, I'm so glad you're home. Now everything is just perfect!" He taps his pipe against an onyx ashtray. "Why don't we order in a pizza with the works while we talk about what we'll do together this summer? Would you like to go the mountains, my darling, or perhaps to the ocean?" And when my mother gets home, he mixes cocktails for them both, rubs her feet, and tells her that dinner is on its way.

MIMI, REAL LIFE

Except for studying, I spent every possible minute of my last year in high school, like the previous years, immersed in one or the other of my fantasies. Céline or the queen or the pageant lady or my dad followed me to school, to the library, to the dentist's office. I was never alone.

My only other pastime was hiding in the washroom, obsessing about my appearance. In an effort to cut down on the heinous crime of Bathroom Loitering, someone on the staff of St. Mary's had removed the mirrors, so I had to contort myself to see my reflection in the shiny steel doors on the cubicles. My reflection looked as distorted as a fun-house mirror, but it was, alas, accurate.

I would squint and try to see a girl who looked like the other girls in my class: the sleek and flossy girls with their coltish legs who pored over magazine articles entitled "Find Your Best Summer Look" (you can bet that isn't my handed-down-from-my-mother flowery muumuu) and "How to Spot a Virgin." (No problem there. Me.) And "Say Yes to Great Skin." (Not if it means saying no to chocolate.)

Even with my stomach sucked in and my back ramrod straight, I did not look like anyone else but me: the only girl at St. Mary's Academy whose dress size matched her age – I was seventeen and, at five foot two, I weighed 170 pounds. The thinking part of my brain that could do algebra in my head and recite whole swaths of Rimbaud's poetry knew that this did not make me a freak. But the reptile part of my brain that reacted like a trained seal to pictures in fashion magazines knew no such thing.

Then someone else would come bustling in, and I would adjust my St. Mary's Academy uniform – a kilt that would have fit Robert the Bruce, my man's white shirt, and my knee socks (which drooped dispiritedly, their elastic but a fond memory) – and make my way into the arena like a reluctant gladiator.

Chapter Two

I don't know what possessed me to go to Prom Night. I would never have willingly hauled my spotty carcass to the school gym, site of countless humiliations at the pommel horse, on the fiendish mats, and at the other instruments of phys ed torture. But the prom was being held at the gorgeous Queen Elizabeth Hotel in downtown Montréal, a place I'd only ever heard of. There would be gilt mirrors hanging from the silk-covered walls, which would reflect the ornate crystal candelabra so that they looked ablaze. There would be thousands and thousands of flowers – sharp and spicy and sweet all at once – nodding in graceful vases. I wanted, craved, some of that sheen. Besides, Queen Elizabeth had been there. I would be looking at the very same walls that she had looked at with her royal eyes.

It's pathetic, but you should know this about me. I like beautiful things. It's not that I want to own them, I just love to look at them. I love horses and the way they shine and Impressionist paintings and stately poppies and pearls. For once I wanted, longed, to be part of the freshly washed, perfumed, graceful crowd on Prom Night.

As soon as I walked into the grand ballroom (theme: Salute to Flowers), I realized I'd made a colossal mistake.

"Ohmigawd!" said Macy. "Is that you, Mimi?" Macy, of the brown satin (black is so yesterday) off-the-shoulder dress, her glossy blonde hair held back by a fresh camellia. Macy, who had never said a civil word to me.

My face was frozen into a frightened half-smile. I was afraid to move in case she struck. Macy was a snake. A snake with the power to make me a laughingstock with the tiniest wry twist of her iridescent mouth.

"It *is* you! I didn't recognize you under all that makeup. Wow, is that nail polish ever red, and the lipstick! Oh, I just love that green dress against your skin. Vintage?"

It was vintage alright. But not in a good way, as Macy well knew. It was my mother's dress from when she was pregnant with me. What had felt silky and sort of Mary Quant Swinging London, with a big pussycat bow under the chin, all of a sudden felt like a deflated parachute.

"It's nice and roomy. Mine's so tight, I don't know how I'll be able to dance." This was clearly not a problem I was going to have to face. I wanted to pry up one of the cabbage roses on the vast rug with my toe and disappear under it. The hopeful makeup felt like mud on my face. What was I thinking? What was I *thinking*?

Macy slid away for a moment, and Akila – best known for her year-round tan – appeared in her place. "Hi, Mimi. Did you see what Macy's wearing? That is the most beautiful dress I've ever seen, ohmigawd!" She gave herself a happy little shake. "What's wrong? You look sort of green."

She turned back to Macy, who had planted herself at the door once again to bestow her presidential blessing on the arrivals. Akila tried to take Macy's hand, but she shook it off.

"Where's Dorian?" asked Akila.

Macy's boyfriend, Dorian, was a model, so the rumor went. Nobody had ever seen him in person.

"Oh, he's on a photo shoot in Florida. He thinks proms are immature."

You learn a lot when you hang out in the washroom as much as I did. The tom-toms were pounding out the message that Dorian had broken up with Macy. Word had it that he dumped her by sending her a text message on her iphone: *In Miami, need space.* As I'm sure Akila would be happy to tell you, Post-it notes are so six breakups ago. Dorian was probably being kind by not wanting to tax Macy's limited vocabulary with anything longer. Akila reached for

Macy's hand again, but Macy pulled away and Akila was left standing alone by the door.

I made my way to a delicate satin-covered chair by the swing door to the kitchen and sat staring at my pink high-heeled sandals. I took stock one more time. I was the grossest butterball, the fattest cow in this stupid please-don't-feed-the-models private school that was paid for by my mother's two thankless nursing jobs. I knew that many of the Macys and the Akilas who terrified me and fascinated me (you know, the kind of girls who look like they just stepped off the assembly line at Mattel) may have been beautiful, but some of them were also cruel and, well, dumb. I wanted to rake Macy's face with my faux nails (Ribald Red, said the bottle), or at least stand up for myself and not let them make me feel so worthless. But would I?

No. Because Big Beluga here was afraid of her own shadow. That's the way I was. Thieves could walk up to the door of our apartment, and I would invite them in, apologizing for the meager haul of electronics. Then I'd tell them, "Thanks, and come again"! For all my size, I was a mouse. A mouse that gobbled cheese. Fattening, runny, delicious cheese.

"Hey, Mimi, good to see you." Mrs. McKnight was balancing a plastic cup full of a neon orange liquid on her clipboard. Mrs. McKnight was sixty-something, the height of the average ten-year-old, with black skin that always smelled faintly of Noxzema. She tied her kinky gray hair back with blue or pink shoelaces. The girls called her *The Hippie* because she looked like one and because she had taped a picture of John Lennon and Yoko Ono on the closet door in her classroom.

Every teacher at St. Mary's Academy had a nickname: *The Fridge* was the icy Mrs. Myrtle, our gym teacher; *The Giraffe* was Mrs. Maurice, who taught French and dressed like a spy from the Second World War, with her no-nonsense shoes and her hair rolled into a sausage over her forehead; and the not-too-subtle *Fairy* was Mr. McTavish, the principal, who Macy had once seen walking hand in hand with another man on a beach in Cuba during March Break. She spread that news fast and poisonously, causing many a self-righteous Parents Association meeting. The furor eventually died down, but the nickname stuck.

Five years ago, when we were in grade seven, Mrs. McKnight caught Macy cheating by copying from Akila's test paper. Zero for both of them. A potential suicidal act for a teacher at a school full of the offspring of *tout* Montréal society, but Mrs. McKnight is brave. That was a great day. Add to that the time when Mrs. McKnight cried as she read us Ophelia's mad scene, and when she didn't laugh at me as I chewed up my English pronunciation (maybe you can't tell just by reading this, but when I try to speak English, I have this *huge* French accent, even thicker than Céline's). I swore silent allegiance to her.

I hauled my yearbook out of my knapsack, which I'd covered in glue-on sequins in the hope that it would look Wacky in a Good Way. Dashed hope. The knapsack looked like what it was: a lumpy stand-in for the delicate jeweled clutches the other girls carried.

"Will you sign it for me?" I handed the yearbook to Mrs. McKnight.

"Of course, my dear. And what a nice pen. Purple ink?"

When she opened the book, her smile disappeared. Wrinkles pursed around her mouth. "When did you get your yearbook?"

"Last week, just like everyone else. . . ."

"It looks like I'm the first to sign it. Well, I consider that an honor." She wrote her name with a flourish.

"You know, Mimi, I've always wanted to say something to you and I guess it's now or never. Listen to me. You are a smart girl and you have incredible potential. I hope you know that and I hope you won't let anyone mess with your talent or your heart. Anyone! And that includes *you.*

Let yourself grow into the person you can be. Do you hear me?" When she said "hear me," she blinked hard.

"Yes," I said doubtfully, bobbing my head like a toy bulldog in the back window of a car. Grow was the last thing I wanted to do.

She handed back the yearbook and crossed the ballroom to take a seat at the teachers' table.

♡

"Good evening, ladies and gentlemen, and welcome to Prom Night." Mr. McTavish rocked back on his white leather shoes and fussed with his pink satin tie. "Girls, I want you all to think about your parents tonight and the prom nights that have preceded this one in our school's proud history."

There wasn't much for *me* to think about. I never knew my dad. The words "father" and "papa" are not part of my vocabulary, except when I am living in my Mimi, the Daughter imaginary world.

"Girls, you've accomplished a lot during your years at school, just like your mothers and grandmothers did before you," he said, voice trembling. "Tonight is *your* night."

Nobody goes to this school alone. They drag along their family trees, full of ancestors who are household names on the stock-market pages and society pages of the newspapers and on the shelves at the supermarket. My poor maman, who knew she couldn't give me a father, worked at two hospitals to pay for me to be here. I made my way to school from our ground-floor rented duplex – not far from where she grew up in Rosemont – and not from one of the grand houses on the mountainside.

As Mr. McTavish droned on, I slipped into make-believe Fatherland. It's my happiest place to be. I've been constructing it all my life. I can't remember when I didn't know that my father was an anonymous sperm donor, when I didn't want to know everything about him, and when I didn't know that there were questions too hurtful to ask.

This is all I had gleaned from years of pestering Maman. She had always wanted to have a child, but her soon-to-be-ex husband did not. At least, not with his wife. When she turned thirty-nine, she divorced the guy, sold the house, colored her hair blonde, and went to a sperm bank in Toronto. Why Toronto? No idea, but I knew her younger sister, Amélie, lived there. My mother doesn't talk much about Amélie, except she once told me that Amélie taught astronomy at the University of Toronto.

"Girls, I'm sure your parents are very proud of you."

I knew Maman was. I never told her what I faced at St. Mary's, but I'm sure she recognized that it was hard for me – she's very smart about most things. But I guess her dream involved giving me a shot at a world populated by the Fine Old Families of Montréal and I wasn't going to be the one to disillusion her. She had put her whole life on hold to give me what she considered my biggest chance. But big as I was, I had grown to feel like an invisible half-person. On the way to the Queen Elizabeth Hotel in my green pouffy dress, my feet pillowing up between the straps of my pink sandals, I had played my favorite game: Is that man with the briefcase my father? What about the one with the folded *La Presse*? Or the one looking at his reflection and picking his teeth, God forbid? I wanted to know. I needed to know.

Mr. McTavish took three small steps back and then a giant step forward. "It's time to introduce a lady who has been a model of leadership and school spirit throughout her academic career. Please welcome Macy Moore!"

Everyone applauded as Macy climbed the steps leading to the stage, except Mrs. McKnight, who was rolling her eyes and sipping from her punch glass. Macy may have been gnashing her perfect white teeth over Dorian, but she looked serene and gorgeous. Mean and gorgeous.

"Thank you, Mr. McTavish, and what a great tie! Ralph Lauren?" Mr. McTavish turned red and backed away. (Good thinking, Mr. McT. Don't turn your back on her.)

"Hi, all! We have a special treat for you tonight. It's a pleasure to host this year's St. Mary's Academy Awards. And to do so, please welcome my cohost, Akila Molson."

Same thing. *Clap clap clap clap clap clap.*

"What an honor to be up here with our queen, Macy, ohmigaaaaaawd!" Akila trailed off into a squeal. (I wanted to yell, *Quick, someone, get the fire hose.* But of course I didn't, and Akila more or less composed herself.)

Our uniforms were supposed to free us from fashion rivalries and make us feel equal. That's rich. All the uniform code achieved was elevating accessories to objects of veneration – your identity was created by your shoes and handbags.

"Our first award is for handbags," Macy announced. "Who had the hottest handbag during the last school year? Our finalists are Alice for her red Hermès, Muriel's Birkin bag, and, of course, Christianne, who blew us all away with her Dooney & Bourke. . . ."

The Prom Night awards covered shoes, cufflinks (we wore shirts, remember), earrings, stockings, hair bands, everything except our kilts, jackets, shirts, and ties. Despite the shrieks of the presenters and the winners, it was stunningly dull. I should have stayed home and listened to my Céline Dion CDs. When I listen to them, I don't care about what I look like, or fingers pointing at me, or people making jokes they think I don't understand – her music makes me free.

I still remember the first time I heard her voice. Maman and I were in the mall, I was maybe seven years old, and it was wintertime. Maman was looking to buy a TV – our first – and on all the screens in the store, there she was: a thin silhouette moving like a swan, her hair floating in the air, and a crystal voice dancing on panpipe music on the *Titanic*. The next three or four minutes were the most moving, inspiring, electrifying, and troubling of my entire life. Something had shifted in my heart, but I couldn't express it with words – it was the same feeling I had when I learned how to read my very first sentence in grade one and could understand the meaning of it, like eating a crème brûlée when the sky above your head is bursting with fireworks and possibilities.

Finally, after many false starts, Mr. McTavish was able to grab the mike. "Well done, girls! That about wraps it –"

Macy took the mike from his hand. "There's one more category," she said firmly. "Perfume!"

"Ohmigawd, no kidding!" said Akila, as if Macy were about to announce a cure for AIDS.

"This is the last award. The finalists for the most unforgettable perfume are – ohmigawd – Akila for Calvin Klein's *Euphoria* because it's really feminine, me for Christian Dior's *Diorissimo* because it smells like carnations, and," she paused for effect, "Mimi!"

The crowd stamped and whistled. I looked around, confused.

"For Preparation H!"

At first, all that registered was my name. The pain followed. I felt as if someone had skewered my heart with two long knitting needles. I stuffed my hand in my mouth to make sure that no sound could seep out and ran as fast as I could. Everyone was looking at me. If Mr. McTavish said anything above the din, I didn't hear it. My pink high-heeled sandal snagged on the rug and broke. I limped into the luxurious women's washroom and huddled on the floor of the handicapped stall.

"Mimi? Mimi?" I felt a hand on my shoulder. I tried to hide my face because I knew my mascara had made black football-player smudges under my eyes.

"Please, leave me alone . . . ," I said.

"I'm so sorry. That girl is so *mean*! She's always been mean, and there's nothing any of us can do to change it."

I recognized Mrs. McKnight's voice. She must have crawled under the door. She was on her knees, rocking me like a baby.

"Why?" That was the only word that came to my mind, and I said it into Mrs. McKnight's shoulder over and over. "What am I going to do? Everyone saw me run away and fall."

"Well, you don't actually have to do anything. The disc jockey's started and everybody's dancing. You can just leave. But I won't let you. I want you to wash your face, go back to that ballroom, and ask for the apology you so royally deserve."

"I can't."

"Not only can you, but you will. Give me your hand!"

"No, please!"

"Look, Mimi. If you leave this school knowing just one thing, it should be this. I know those girls have colluded to make you miserable. That's done. But don't be part of the plot. Don't let other people define who you are! You have to write your own story if you are going to be truly happy in this life. Now haul your sorry self on up."

She helped me pull off my other sandal and hoisted me to my feet. She ran water in the sink and washed my face with one of the hotel's scented fake-cloth towels.

With every wipe and pat, Mrs. McKnight grumbled her outrage. "Spoiled brats! And they look ridiculous. 'Look at me, Akila! I've got breasts!' 'Me, too, Macy. I'm so empowered. It's not about attracting males, no, no, it's about taking control of my own, like, destiny.' 'Yeah, like, doesn't that make me special?' And that wimpy, boot-licking McTavish. . . ." When she was finished, we both plunked down companionably on the marble floor.

It was the first time I'd ever heard Mrs. McKnight say anything like that. I loved it and wanted more. She smiled and I laughed with relief.

"Oh, look at you, laughing now. I wanted to hear that laugh so badly, dear. Those girls don't deserve a single one of your tears."

"You're right." I wiped my nose on my bow.

"I'm no fortune-teller, but there are some things I can predict. I have a hunch which of you has a shot at calculating pi, or helping to save the rainforest, or addressing the United Nations in a closed session, or negotiating a peace treaty in the Middle East, or discovering a cure for gingivitis, or just being a good, caring adult. And my money's not on Macy or Akila."

"How do you know?"

"It's hard to do any of that stuff when you're fixated on text-messaging your friends about a pair of shoes you *have* to have and choosing the right facial exfoliant. Or you'll just die, ohmigawd."

I laughed again, and so did Mrs. McKnight.

"Are you ready?" She was struggling to her feet.

"For what?"

"For your punch-up with Macy."

I looked up at her as she held out her hand to me.

"I'm just kidding, honey, although it's not that I wouldn't love to see it. Seriously, I want her to apologize to you."

"Mrs. McKnight, I just want to go home."

She must have recognized the mulelike quality I could summon for such occasions because she said, "I can't force you to do something you don't want to do. Do you need a ride?"

"Thank you. Thank you very much."

We went out a side exit so I wouldn't have to face anybody. Mrs. McKnight drove me home in her old blue Toyota. She had the radio blaring "Come On (Let the Good Times Roll)," and we didn't even try to talk.

Chapter Three

*M*aman was hovering at the door, a mug of hot chocolate in her hand, as I turned the key. Her eager face sagged as she studied mine.

"What happened? Your eyes are red. And where are your shoes?"

"Maman, just leave me alone, *s'il te plaît.*"

"Mimi, talk to me. *Dis à maman.* It breaks my heart when I see you like this."

I couldn't bear her pain as well as my own. I ran down the hall to my bedroom and closed the door behind me. Her tired voice followed me. "I'm here for you, Mimi, and I always will be. We're a team, you and me!"

I unzipped the green dress and it fell in a puddle at my ankles. I turned to my mirror, half-naked. I stared at my straight straw hair, the scars left from my bout with chicken pox, my legs, my hips, by big butt, my stomach, my breasts, and my face, as if they belonged to someone else. I looked like a middle-aged woman who had let herself go – my maman, in fact. Every part of me was extralarge. She and I were two super-dressed extralarge pizzas – the kind that could feed ten thousand. There was flab under my arms and on my butt. I had two chins. I looked like a Cabbage Patch Kid, but not as cute. I touched my breasts and my belly. The flesh felt like Jell-O – it moved around, and I could squeeze it with my fingers.

"Where do you come from, you bouncy castle?" (The inflatable toy – the bouncy castle – at day care had been my favorite place in the whole world until I outgrew it.)

Was my father fat like me, or was he slim? Were my father's eyes blue like mine? Did he have other children, and did they look like me? Had he been a med student who needed money to pay his tuition, or some lazy jerk who couldn't be bothered getting a real job? What does it matter, if you're too chicken to try to find out?

I thought of Mrs. McKnight's laugh. She would hate this scene.

"Okay, Mimi, snap out of it! You're a smart person. If you could just get over worrying about what other people think of you, you could do anything. Don't let anyone mess with your talent or your heart."

I took stock. Maman had handed me a life, but I hadn't used it yet – it was still in its plastic wrapping. I was making the girl in the mirror cry. That infuriated me. Suddenly, I was tired. I fished around for one of my fantasies, but I couldn't conjure up Céline, or the queen, or the beauty pageant. *Quit it! Nobody's going to live your life for you. You are the biggest coward in the whole wide world. If you're so obsessed with your father, go find him!*

PRACTICAL MIMI
Is now the time to mention the practicalities? This is why I couldn't find my father.

1. I had just graduated from high school with a fistful of acceptances to good universities. I'd narrowed it down to McGill, so I could live at home. Why pay for housing?
2. The sperm bank was in Toronto and the idea of traveling far from Montréal terrified me. People might laugh at my English or at my size.
3. Maman would never let me go.

I unbuttoned my Persian-kitten pajama bag and shook out my nightgown. It had ruffles and buttons all down the front (I suspect it was actually for nursing mothers), and the soft cotton always gave me a little shiver of pleasure. I opened the drawer of my bedside table and ran my fingers over my stock of chocolate bars. *Aha! I believe Madame will be having a Hershey's this evening!* I've learned not to feel guilty ever since I read that dark chocolate has more antioxidants – they destroy free radicals that can damage cells and contribute to disease – than red wine or berries.

I pulled back the comforter and arranged the pillows. But, oddly enough, something stopped me before I could unwrap the candy. An unfamiliar voice had stirred in me: *Mimi, put that chocolate bar back!* I did as I was told and slept for twelve hours.

Chapter Four

When I opened my eyes, the sun was beating in through the window. I could hear the midday sounds of the street. Maman was sitting on my bed, a forced smile stretching her cheeks.

"How are you, *chérie*? Sleep well?"

"Okay. *Comme ci comme ça.*"

"I made crepes for breakfast. Do you want them with the works? I've got sour cream."

I wanted to tell her, *Maman, look at me! Do you really think I need more fat?* but I never "talked fat" with her. She always rewarded me with food when I was a kid. As far as I remember, she put honey on my pacifier and, later, gave me Little Debbie snack cakes after school every time I got an A+. And I got plenty of them.

"What's wrong, Mimi? *Qu'est-ce qui s'est passé?*"

"Maman, can we not talk about it?"

Maman shifted her bulk and the bed creaked. She was the size of a Smart Car, but she hadn't always been overweight. I'd seen pictures. She used to be normal. I was too, until I turned twelve and went from what the kids called carpenter's delight, flat as a board, to a ship with a huge prow. All this happened when Maman had slated me for Greater Things at St. Mary's. I guess the apple (or is it the apple strudel?) doesn't fall very far from the tree.

"Mrs. McKnight phoned. She told me what happened."

I covered my ears with my hands.

"Mimi, please, *écoute bien*."

I couldn't help it. I crossed my arms and looked at the ceiling, wishing her to vanish.

"Mrs. McKnight told me that the girls were mean to you and –"

"Please, Maman! I don't need you to tell me what they did. I was there, remember?"

Maman took me in her arms, and I could feel her tears dampening the top of my head.

"I'm so sorry, *chérie*," she said. "It's all my fault. There is so much I couldn't give you, but I wanted you to have a real chance."

"It's okay, Maman. *Ça ne fait rien.* I guess there are mean girls everywhere. They aren't the ones that stuffed me full of food. I managed that myself."

She smoothed my hair.

"Maman, there's something I want to tell you." The room, with its pink striped paper and posters of Monet's *Water Lilies* framed in silk, seemed stifling and small.

"*Oui, chérie?*"

"You know I love you, right?"

"Okay, what's up?"

I didn't really have a plan until I started to talk, and then it fell into place, as if I had been thinking about it for months. "I want to go to Toronto for the summer."

"Whatever for?"

"To find the donor." (I never used the word "father" in front of her.)

"But what about your plans for the summer?"

"Maman, my plans consist of pouring coffee at Herta's and reading ahead for my courses. I can pour and read in Toronto."

She picked at the crocheted throw at the foot of the bed. "I don't understand. Why is finding him so important to you?"

"I don't know. Maybe because with it being just you and me, I'm scared about what would happen if you were gone. That would leave me with nobody. Grandma and Grandpa died when you were sixteen, and you don't even talk to Tante Amélie."

That was the best I could do. In truth, I didn't know why. I just knew that I felt like I was scrambled inside and that I had to take a step outside of this room, this life, if I was ever going to put myself in order.

She stood up and looked at me as if I were a stranger.

But I was on a roll. I couldn't stop myself. "Why don't you ever talk about Tante Amélie? What happened between you? She's the only family you have left." Tante Amélie was a subject almost as sensitive and off-limits as my donor-father.

"*You* are the only family I have left, Mimi, and that's always been enough for me. I thought it was enough for you too."

"There's got to be more than this."

♡

Maman had the day off. The discussion went on and on, right through the day-long, end-of-term sorting out of school artifacts – the kilt with its ink stains, the report cards, the essays. We'd be talking about safe things, like what to keep and what to ditch, and then the subject would resurface.

"You can't go to Toronto. There's crime there. Besides, all they speak is English."

"*Je parle anglais* (sort of). That's why you sent me to St. Mary's, remember? And it's not like there's no crime here."

"What would you do? I can't afford to support you. Everything I have saved up is for your tuition."

"I'll get a job."

"I know! What if we go there together and spend a week sightseeing? That'll be a nice change."

"Why? *Pourquoi?*"

"Because you can't go there alone. Don't you read the newspapers? Girls get kidnapped by crazy people."

"The whole point is for me to go alone. *I have to try my wings.*"

Maman finished taping up a cardboard box and was writing MEMENTOS — MIMI on it with Magic Marker. "Is that from a song of Céline Dion?"

♡

Later I found her sitting at the kitchen table. Everything was clean and shiny and white and ordered. She had put freshly cut tulips in a vase. Her eyes were puffy. She started in again.

"You have everything you need right here. You can work just down the street, and you can read all you like without a thought about laundry or groceries, just your books."

"I need a break. I don't want books, I want people."

"Do you think that things will really be different there? People can be cruel, you know." With her finger, Maman traced a flower on the linen placemat in front of her.

"All I know is, I am the most clueless, frightened person in the world." Now I was crying.

"You are not! Mrs. McKnight told me that you were one of the best students she's ever taught. Doesn't that mean anything to you, Mimi?"

"I won't go forever. I'll be back for university. I promise."

"The answer is no."

"I'm seventeen, almost eighteen. You can't stop me *tout le temps!*" I grabbed the sponge on the edge of the sink and scrubbed at an imaginary spot on the tile backsplash.

"As long as you stay *chez moi*, you will do what I want you to do." We both knew that was a lame threat, and I ignored it.

"I want to know who he is, Maman. What do you know about him? Please, I need to know. Something. Anything."

"Stop it!"

"If this were a hundred years ago, I'd be married and a mother by now. I'm not your baby anymore."

"I have had all I can take of this conversation," said Maman. She picked up her purse and her jacket and slammed the door, for the first time I could recall. I went into my bedroom and rifled through my Céline Dion CDs.

Mimi and Céline

We are sitting at the side of the pool on a scorching hot Las Vegas day. I am wearing a bikini. Céline is feeling down. "Why does somebody as smart as you like me, Mimi?"

"Well, obviously there's your voice, but also you come from the same background as me. Your family is poor, and your English used to be sketchy. Now, look at you. You're a star, almost a queen. And you're thin, so thin. You really should eat more."

♡

The phone rang just as I heard Maman's key in the door. She brushed by me to answer it. I could tell that her eyes were raw. All I could hear of her conversation was "Yes, *hm, hm,*" and "I'll think about it, thank you."

With deliberate motions, she hung up her jacket and straightened it on the hanger. She stepped out of her shoes and lined them up precisely on the closet floor. I watched, fascinated to see how she could draw out these simple acts. Finally she turned to me.

"Mimi, please sit down. I have something I want to tell you." She sat in her reclining chair and motioned at the couch.

I hated when she acted like that. Without fail, I thought that the world was coming to an end.

Although it never was, my clenching stomach made me sure that it had to be catastrophic news: "*Mimi, I have only three more months to live,*" or, "*I've embezzled the petty cash from the hospital, and I'm going to leave you for a stint in prison.*"

"Mimi, you know money has been tight. I don't want you to have to scrimp while you're at university, so I've applied for a live-in nursing assignment. I won't have to rush between two hospitals, and the pay is wonderful. But there's a catch. It's in the Îles de la Madeleine. . . ."

The islands are in the Gulf of St. Lawrence – much closer to Prince Edward Island than to Montréal. In other words, far away and hard to get to.

"I would be doing home nursing for an old woman there. She has Alzheimer's. I thought they had hired someone else, but they've offered me the job. The contract starts next week and ends in September. It would mean extra money, but the only thing is, I'd be leaving you here alone. We haven't been apart, ever, except when you went on that school trip and the time you went to camp in the Laurentians, and you know how that turned out."

I did. She had to come and pick me up when I set a camp record for crying from home-sickness.

"Is that it?" I said. (Compared to embezzlement or imminent death, this was not big news.)

"Yes. Is that okay with you? I thought it would be a good idea. I've never been to the Îles de la Madeleine, and they are supposed to be lovely. And I would see the ocean. It's something I've always longed to do. Maybe we could each use a little space, don't you think? And when I am back, maybe we'll see things in a different way. Maybe you'll realize that knowing about the sperm donor is not so important." She sounded so wistful, so eager for me to say it was okay, that I thought my heart would break.

"Maybe" was all I could say. During our entire conversation, she hardly lifted her eyes from the perfectly stacked pile of crossword-puzzle books we keep on the coffee table.

Chapter Five

Maman had a week to get ready and she was frantic. She packed and re-packed her suitcases and then she packed and repacked the car. She would drive right through Québec and New Brunswick, then catch the ferry from Prince Edward Island. It would take a couple of days. There was much checking of schedules and poring over maps, but she spent the longest time choosing CDs to play in the car. All the while, she asked me over and over if I didn't mind staying at home by myself.

As for me, I assured her I'd be fine. I was the most self-sufficient person on the planet. I went to the Westmount Public Library to stock up on magazines about the British monarchy, full of more details of royal headgear than any normal person would ever need to know. I assured Maman that I would go for a walk every day. And we agreed that I'd work at Brock's Pub and Grub, in the strip mall close to our apartment.

Brock's Pub and Grub was a misnomer on several counts. There was no Brock (the owner's name was Herta), there was no grub, unless you count fly-specked muffins, and it was far from being a pub. All Herta served was coffee, tea, and abuse, which she lavished on her staff as well as her customers. Not surprisingly, the HELP WANTED notice in the window was a permanent fixture. I knew that I could just turn up and I'd have a job. Street lore was, if you can walk and talk, you can work at Brock's.

As Maman got ready, I spent most of the time in my bedroom with the door closed – listening to Céline, or reading about royal hats, or sketching gowns for the Miss Never Neverland contest I was always imagining. Or all three.

♡

The drone of the vacuum cleaner, the pounding of rugs, and the sloshing of the mop finally stilled. There wasn't a square inch of the apartment left to vacuum, or to wash, or to dust. I was in my room, not wanting to disturb the Domestic Perfection that had been achieved beyond my door, when Maman tapped gingerly.

I was lying on top of my pink cotton sheets, pinned to my bed by the heat, when she came into my room.

"I would like to give you a hug before I go," she said stiffly. The formality didn't fool me. I could tell she was fighting back tears. She handed me a ring binder with tabs reading

EMERGENCY HOME, EMERGENCY HEALTH, HOUSE, MONEY, and CONTACTS. There was a section for cooking, for laundry, for the disposal of different kinds of garbage.

"Here are all the phone numbers – the house in the Îles de la Madeleine, the clinic there, the doctor there, the doctor here." She had filled the sleeves with coupons for take-out food and with Post-its, reminding me not to let any delivery boys into the house. It must have taken her hours to compile. In her flowery hand, she had written an entire manual for surviving a summer in the wilds of Montréal. Here are the highlights:

MIMI'S SURVIVAL MANUAL

1. Don't forget to lock the door when you leave or when you go to bed.
2. Go straight to the bank with your paycheck.
3. Use my debit card. I have made sure there's enough money for groceries.
4. Turn off the oven when you're done with it, and don't leave the water running in the bath. Unplug all the electrical appliances when you leave the apartment, in case there is a storm and we're hit by lightning.

5. Don't listen to Céline all day long.
   Try to go outside and take a walk *every
   single day*.
6. Remember that I love you and I'll see
   you in September.

She kissed me on the forehead and gently put her warm hand on my left cheek. I noticed the deep blue veins coursing through the top of her hand. She tried to smile. Neither one of us spoke. I padded after her into the kitchen and watched her pick up a stray crumb that sat on the immaculate tile counter. We said teary, brusque good-byes. "Don't come out to the car with me, *chérie*. I'll worry that you got locked out."

I ran to the living-room window. Maman was looking up at the harsh gray summer sky dreamily. For the first time in my life, she seemed separate from me. How was it that she could have her own dreams? Despite her size, she looked frail as she reached for her yellow-and-green overnight case. I watched her stow it in the trunk between her suitcases and green garbage bag containing her quilt and pillows. She turned and waved. I waved back, and she smiled and blew me a kiss.

♡

I watched until the car had melted into the traffic. Slowly I started to get dressed. Cargo pants, a loose blouse that billowed over the wide pants, and a pair of my mother's nursing clogs. Not fetching, but practical, in case Herta put me to work right away. I double-checked that I'd locked the door behind me and stepped onto the street. The shining flecks of mica in the sidewalk made my eyes ache.

When I got to the small, sad collection of stores — a dry cleaner, a convenience store specializing in the sale of cigarettes to minors, a Laundromat, a store that sold lead soldiers to collectors, and the Palais des Pooches — it took me a moment to realize that something was different.

One of the dog washers was holding a leash and making encouraging noises to a portly spaniel. "Make a nice go-go, Bluebell," she said patiently. Bluebell ignored her.

"Excuse me. Sorry to interrupt." The woman snorted. "What happened to the Pub and Grub? It looks like it's gone."

"That's the new incarnation." She motioned with the leash.

The new incarnation was too cool to have a sign I could read. When I looked carefully, I saw that the word "need" was etched into a corner, and that was it. In the few days I'd been at home, an exotic flower had appeared on the block. I opened the door and was met by the smell of fresh paint. The floor was black and white, and a gorgeous copper espresso-maker sat on the marble counter. The ceiling was ornate pressed tin. The booths were gone, replaced by marble tables and café chairs. A blackboard on the wall read "You need . . ." and listed an array of what I could only guess were different kinds of coffee.

Behind the counter was a girl my age. Despite the heat, she wore black suede boots, a black dress, long black lace gloves full of deliberate snags, and a chain of barbed wire tattooed around her neck. She stood silently, waiting for me to speak.

"I've come to see about a job," I said. "Can I see the manager?"

"I'm the manager," she said.

I backed out, bewildered, and turned to go home.

♡

To understand how bizarre, how unexpected, what happened next was, you have to realize that I am not an impetuous person. The word "slug" has been a recurring theme in my life. Call it inertia, but I've never seen myself as much of a traveler. The only time I'd been out of Québec was for a school trip to Ottawa. Going on a bus crowded with St. Mary's girls to see the Parliament Buildings and the Canadian Museum of Civilization is hardly what you'd call adventure travel, unless you count the mountains of luggage as natural wonders. So you can understand what a huge whale of a plan seemed to materialize out of nowhere and sweep me along with it. The possibility of wearing my mother's sensible shoes while I poured acrid coffee and wiped sticky counters at the Pub and Grub had evaporated. By the time I got home, I realized that I was free. There was only one thing to do. I would spend the next two months in Toronto, trying to find my father.

I had hardly ever disobeyed Maman. There was nothing big we disagreed about, and the rest seemed like too much trouble to fight about. And it certainly had never before occurred to me to disobey her on such a gargantuan level. I was amazed at how easily I could convince myself that it was okay. All I had to do was tell myself that she would not even have to know. I had a cell phone and could keep in touch with her as easily as if I were in Montréal.

Once the idea came to me, I felt as if I had seconds to act, instead of days or weeks. I ran to Maman's bedroom. She had left it as ordered as a hospital room, the bed linens stretched into unforgiving precision and the smell of lemon wax rising from every wooden surface. After much muttering, sighing, and opening and closing of drawers, I went into the kitchen holding two envelopes.

One held an official-looking form and several duplicates. Across the top was written *Sperm Donor ID: Toronto Cryobank THEO-1*. The other envelope contained a note. I smoothed it out: *For Mimi when I die. The day has come for you to know.* I read the page twice. There was a lot of information, including an address in Toronto and a doctor's name. I had hit the jackpot! I don't remember ever feeling so happy.

I had a knack for remembering the tiniest of historical details about various military campaigns, a talent that caused much mirth among my classmates at St. Mary's. But all those details of all those military campaigns proved to be of use. I set to work.

I tore a piece of paper out of the household binder so lovingly prepared by Maman and plotted my conquest of Toronto. I got my atlas and spread it out on the kitchen table.

MIMI'S CAMPAIGN
How was I going to get to Toronto, approximately 350 miles away? *By bus.*

What would I use for money? *I'd take as much as I dared at one time out of the bank machine and the rest would have to be from the small bursary I won at school.*

Where would I stay? *Tante Amélie's?*

How would I deal with my poor English? *By using my French-English dictionary.*

How would I find my father? *I had the cryobank address. Surely, surely, that would be enough.*

I am my mother's daughter, so I also made a list of possible snags and a list of solutions. What if Maman phoned one of the neighbors and asked after me? What if she came home early? What if pipes burst, or the apartment caught on fire, or the street blew up? The list of solutions remained blank. All the while, I was making plans. I knew it was crazy, but deep down, I hoped that my sperm donor – Dad – would be there, waiting for me.

♡

After I made my bed, hospital corners and all, and dusted my desk – under a shelf of books, neatly arranged by author in alphabetical order – I went to the jumble drawer in the kitchen, the only few square inches in the whole apartment where there was chaos among the bits of string, batteries, old birthday candles, and matches, and I found Maman's old address book. I looked under the letter *M* for Amélie Morissette. Her name was there, but the address and the phone number were blacked out.

I had planned to spend the rest of the day indoors, within reach of our halfhearted air conditioner, but the inked-out address intrigued me. I pulled on a loose T-shirt and shorts and stepped back out into the steaming day. The library was full of people waiting out the heat, and there was a lineup for each computer. Eventually it was my turn, and I went on-line to find my aunt. After trying five times, here's what I got: *We're sorry. Your search returned no results. Please verify that your information was entered correctly, or try again with a broader range of search information.* A challenge. I went into the website of the University of Toronto's Department of Astronomy and Astrophysics, and not only did I find her name, e-mail address, phone number, and photograph (she looked like Maman, but a much slimmer version), but I also read about her research interests, her papers in journals such as "The Globular Cluster Omega Centauri and the Origin of the Oosterhoff Dichotomy," and the courses she taught like AST310H2 – Great Moments in Astronomy. I scribbled everything down.

Finding the information about Tante Amélie seemed like a sign that my plan was plausible and real. It filled me with a sense of purpose, foreign to me and very sweet. I could have danced home from the library, but, of course, I didn't. I could just imagine myself, a dancing cow, galumphing merrily down the street. I stopped for a moment under the shade of the Chocolaterie's green awning. The Chocolaterie is the best candy store in Montréal and, as far as I'm concerned, the best in the galaxy. The chocolates in the glass cases were gorgeous, dazzling, perfect.

MIMI AND CHOCOLATE

A neat arrangement of ornate blue-silk, butterfly-shaped boxes of truffles beckoned me. I chose the biggest box and took my place in line. While I waited for a small boy to tell his grandmother which piece he wanted from the array behind the glass counter, I nudged open the truffle box. What about a milk-chocolate shell that melts away to a creamy mousselike center? Even better, a mild, airy ganache beneath dark chocolate, adorned with a cascading milk-chocolate finish? *God! You* do *exist!* I was in heaven. The box was full of truffles. Creamy truffles. Truffles crunchy with nuts. Truffles infused with a whisper of raspberry or orange. Truffles featuring a cool white-chocolate filling, with bits of crystallized ginger.

One after another, I gently placed the little wonders in my mouth. At first, it was one at a time, then two, so that my whole mouth was awash with the sweetness. At the end, I was popping them faster. By the time the boy was done (he chose a dark chocolate, caramel-covered and sprinkled with *fleur de sel*), a dozen of the adorable little truffles had disappeared.

"Will that be debit or credit card?" A disinterested woman in a white coverall was speaking to me. I came to. "That's $325.00. Those truffles are handmade, and it's an oak presentation box under all that silk."

I could barely process the words. All I could think of was the expression "My jaw hit the floor." That's what I felt like. Not only my jaw, but everything that gravity affects – including my knees and my arms, but most of all, my fat. I felt as if all of me was one big stupid puddle.

I started to cry. I saw from the saleswoman's expression that she was thinking, *No wonder she's a tub. She eats like a pig!* And the sad part was, she was right. I had eaten up half of my bursary and all of my bus ticket to Toronto.

♡

The minute I stepped into my bedroom, I barfed. If there was a contest for cosmic barfing of Niagara Falls proportions, I would have won it, hands down. I vomited on my papers and on the cargo pants and sweater that I had left balled-up on the floor. I was a mess. I loathed myself. How could I possibly have thought that I could get myself to Toronto? Too much stomach and not enough brains. I scrambled to find a comforting fantasy – my father wiping my sweaty face with a cool cloth, Queen Elizabeth offering me iced ginger ale – but even Céline Dion couldn't do a thing to comfort me.

Eventually, I calmed down. I tried to wipe the vomit off the sheaf of documents about the sperm bank. I put them in the pantry, so they would dry properly, and I put the clothes in a plastic bag and went back out into the heat to the Laundromat.

For some reason, I thought that my sweater could be washed in hot water. When I fished it out, it was Barbie-doll size. I checked the label: HAND WASH IN COLD WATER. Monique, the woman who works at the Laundromat dispensing soap and making sure that nobody turns violent when a machine has one of its regular breakdowns, saw me staring morosely at my ruined sweater.

"It's a knit and might give a bit if you block it out," she said kindly.

As I tried to tug it back into shape at the folding table, I wondered how many hours were left in the wretched day. I turned to look at the clock, when something caught my eye on the bulletin board. I had never paid much attention to it, uninterested as I was in the normal array of notices about furniture for sale, palm-reading services, or Mom and Tot music groups. But this time, a neatly printed card stood out: *Looking for a third person for a ride-share Montréal-Toronto. Please call Fred and Denise.*

"Monique, do you know anything about this?"

"Sure. They're my parents. They're getting a bit creaky, and they like to have someone along to help keep them awake. *Ha-ha-ha!* Actually, they just need someone to help read the map and navigate once the signs are in English. No kidding."

I wrote the number on the back of my hand. This had to be an omen.

♡

When I got home, there was a phone message from Maman. She was at a highway stop, but she sounded as excited as if she had just landed in Paris.

"Nothing special to report," she said, "just be a good girl, and don't let anything Herta says get you down. It's only a summer job. I'll call again when I get to the ferry."

I went into my bedroom, picked up my pink phone, and dialed Fred and Denise's number. After three rings, an old woman answered. Her tremulous voice was hoarse. She spoke hesitantly, but she asked question after question (I guess wanting to reassure herself that I wasn't an ax murderer). Clearly, frequenting the Laundromat where her daughter worked was not enough of a reference. Eventually she wound down, and we settled on a price for the return trip. We'd be gone for a week.

Denise explained that she and Fred were leaving for Toronto the next morning at seven o'clock, and no, she didn't want to pick me up because the part of Montréal in which we lived was too confusing and she'd never find the apartment.

"How long do you think it will take us?" I asked.

"Monique claims it takes six hours, but you know what a madcap she is!"

I did not know. I did a quick count. If we left at seven, we'd be there sometime in the early afternoon.

I was too excited to be frightened. I called Tante Amélie's work number. Her message directed all summer students to take note of her office hours: *four o'clock to six o'clock every afternoon.* Perfect. She was in the city for the summer. I hadn't let myself even consider that she might be on holiday until I almost sobbed with relief. I didn't leave a message. *Hi, I'm your long-lost niece, here to spend a week with you* seemed like the kind of message you should deliver in person. I'd get to the city in lots of time to find her office, introduce myself, and ask her if I could stay with her.

I stuffed my backpack with a couple of T-shirts (including one that sported Monet's *Water Lilies*), jeans, underwear, socks, and two of my favorite CDs – *Falling into You* and *A New Day Has Come*, both by Céline – and two or three chocolate bars, the picture of Maman and me taken at an ice-cream stand in Old Montréal, nail polish, and my toothbrush.

I was afraid, more afraid than I'd ever been in my life. I felt as if my mind was split down the middle like an avocado (my favorite fruit when it is slathered with mayonnaise). I wanted to leave all those years of humiliation, embarrassment, and shame and all those cries of *Look at the Big Cow, Fat Ass, Winnebago Girl* I had heard all through my years at school. Those were the *push* reasons. The *pull* reason was *Sperm Donor ID: Toronto Cryobank THEO-1*.

I once watched a special on giants of the sea. Apparently sharks have to keep moving all the time. I had been still so long that, now that I had found some momentum, I simply could not stop.

Chapter Six

I turned on the TV to keep me company while I went around the apartment checking the windows and unplugging the toaster. The jaunty weather girl was crouched on a sidewalk, showing us that it was "hot enough to fry an egg." I locked the door, stuck a note in the mailbox asking the postman to hold our mail, and set out for the subway with my knapsack on my back.

Fred and Denise lived past the last station of the subway line in a trim bungalow. I saw their old car – an ancient Datsun – in the driveway, its doors and windows open. They were loading the car, one small item at a time. Fred's face cascaded in wrinkles and he looked like a deflating balloon. Denise was as thin as a toothpick. I was taller by far than either of them. It wasn't until I realized how much stronger I was than my minia-ture chauffeurs that it finally dawned on me what trouble I could have been in. I didn't need to be Einstein, or have a mother as protective as mine, to know that going in a car with perfect strangers was not the best idea I'd ever had.

We sized one another up and came to the

mutual conclusion that nobody was a potential kidnapper or kidnappee.

"Would you like to stow your backpack in the trunk?" asked Fred.

"*Non, merci.*" I thought that if I had to make a run for it, at least I'd have a change of clothes.

"I hope you don't mind, but we won't be stopping until we're halfway, around Kingston, so if you'd like to use the lavatory, dear, now's the time to do it." Denise beamed at me and gave a little encouraging cough.

I told her I was fine, and I crawled into the narrow backseat with a map of Québec and a map of Ontario. Denise took the wheel. The first thirty minutes were fine. She knew her way out of the city. Then Fred lit a cigarette. Denise and I took turns coughing in the confines of the small car.

The road between Montréal and Toronto is more or less one straight line (for those of you who don't know). There are no turnoffs. Navigating the route does not require much of a sense of direction. Nevertheless, every time we came to a bypass, and there were plenty of them, Denise would take her eyes from the road, twist in her seat, and ask me which way we should go. And every time, I assured her that we should follow the signs to Toronto. Straight, straight, and straight some more. These exchanges enlivened what has to be one of the most boring stretches of road in the world.

I was fascinated by the speedometer. The pointer never varied. Recreational vehicles hauling boats behind them sped by us. A school bus full of old people beeped at us to get out of the way. I didn't want to rattle Denise because she seemed to be growing more confident. We'd passed the exit to Cornwall, and she had announced triumphantly, "I guess I just keep going straight!" Nevertheless, I asked, "Do you think we'll get to Toronto in the afternoon?" I had to find Tante Amélie's office by six o'clock or I'd be in trouble.

Denise wiggled around to give me her full attention. "Why, I don't know." She sounded as if I were asking a riddle. "Tell me, Mimi, why are you going to Toronto?"

She didn't sound particularly interested. She knew, and I knew, that this was an *I'm-talking-to-a-teenager-and-I-can't-think-of-a-thing-to-say* question.

"Well, *um* . . . I'm going to visit my father. He's going to meet me." As I said it, I realized that it was true.

"That's nice. He lives there, does he?"

"Yes, he owns a construction company. He says that business is better in Toronto."

I have no idea why I added this. I didn't really care if they knew anything about me, and besides, if they were interested, they could easily find out all the juicy details of my thrilling life from Monique, who had been at the Laundromat as long as I could remember. I think I just wanted to try out my fantasy of having a real live father. I once read in a book – the kind you find in the self-help section – that if you visualize enough, or even say out loud what you want, it has more chance of happening. I tried it once. I thought really, really hard about having free tickets to a Céline Dion concert, hoping that I was emitting a magnetic signal to the cosmos that would make it happen. It didn't. I can't say I was surprised. I don't really believe in that stuff. But when Denise asked, I was ready to do anything to find my father, even if it meant lying to a perfectly nice couple. So, I went on and on about my fictional father, as if he were waiting in his living room in Toronto for me to arrive.

"Does he like it there?"

"Yes, he does. I mean, he likes to do business there, but he prefers Montréal," I said.

"Montréal is such a nice city," Denise replied, and abruptly pulled into the right-hand lane to let a trailer full of horses go by.

"And what about you? Why are you going to Toronto?" I asked.

"Our son lives there. And we love adventure! We go to see him for a week every summer." She waved at the driver of the horse trailer as he passed us, leaning on his horn.

And you can't find the way? I thought, but all I said was, "That's great."

"He has two lovely children," Denise continued, "but, my, they are so noisy. So we stay in a hotel downtown. Don't we, dear?" She looked at Fred for approval. He nodded glumly. "Do you have brothers and sisters?" Denise asked.

"No, I don't. Well, both of my parents work, and they just didn't have much time to have kids. My dad travels a lot because of his work, and so does my mom. I guess it would be nice to have siblings, when I get older and both my parents die, but I'm an only child." *Who was saying all this?* Not the Mimi I knew.

"What does your mother do?"

"She's one of the inventors of the Post-it. She's everywhere. I mean, she travels so much, it's not even funny, but, fortunately, I had a nanny to take care of me when I was a kid."

How many lies did I tell? I don't have enough fingers and toes to count them. *Fais attention.* I felt drunk. Not that I have first-hand knowledge of feeling drunk. But the lying was making me giddy.

"What gave your mother the idea of the Post-it?"

"*Uh*, well, that's really funny. I was maybe three years old, I don't remember, but my mom used to write things on her hands that she would forget, and, one day, she had this big skin infection. I mean, her body was red and itchy all over, and the doctor told her that she had to stop writing stuff on her hands because she was allergic to ink. That's how she got the Post-it idea."

"For some reason, I thought Post-its were invented by an American." That was from Fred.

"My mom is American. Yeah, she, *uh*, moved to Montréal when she was sixteen. Her family comes from San Francisco. My grandparents still live there. It's gorgeous, I just love that city. I go visit them every Christmas. My mom has a jet, I mean, a private jet, you know, so it's faster."

"Why didn't you use your mom's private jet to go to Toronto?"

"*Uh*, her jet is being overhauled. She . . . *uh*, she used it too many times, and the motor, I think, has to be changed, yeah . . . so, that's why I . . . I needed a share-ride."

I sounded like an idiot. For a person who has created a whole galaxy of secret lives, it turns out that I am really bad at being a liar. I loved making up the story about my parents (don't get me wrong). But, all along, I knew it was preposterous. Luckily, Denise and Fred had stopped listening to me. The road signs were coming fast and furious, and I had to step up my reassurances that the many signs pointing to Toronto actually meant that we were headed there.

I don't know how long we'd been on the road, but eventually Denise pulled into a highway rest stop that smelled of fried food and diesel. I filled up the gas tank for her, assured her that we were headed west, folded myself into the backseat, closed my eyes, and fell asleep.

Céline Dream

I am in a GAP in downtown Montréal, standing in front of a display wall stacked with jeans. Céline's beside me.

"Those all look like they'd be too big for you. What size are you looking for?" she says.

"Should I be looking at small, maybe?"

"Sure! Actually, I think X-small would fit you better. . . ."

"Yeah. I think so too."

I am standing in line, waiting to get into the fitting room, when a hand pats my shoulder.

♡

"Mimi? Final stop! We're here! Wake up!"

I opened my eyes. Fred was leaning over me. I noticed that two of his side teeth were missing.

"I've been trying to wake you up for ages. And, my goodness, you snore to beat the band!"

"Where am I?"

"You're in Toronto, at the corner of Yonge and Bloor," Denise said, from the driver's seat. "You said your father would meet you here. Would you like us to wait with you?"

"Thanks, no. No."

"You're blocking the intersection! Tourists!" We were parked under a NO-STANDING sign at the busiest intersection in the country. A man dressed in a suit walked in front of the car and pounded his fist on the hood.

Fred's joints creaked as he got out to open the door for me. I grabbed my backpack as cars whizzed by, honking their horns at us. Fred was unfazed. He shook my hand good-bye. "See you same time next week. Here's our number if anything changes. Good luck, girlie. You'll need it." Before I could ask him what he meant, Denise gunned the motor and they were gone.

♡

Yonge and Bloor at rush hour. There were giant screens flashing ads on the roofs of the buildings and hot-dog vendors at all four corners. The sky was blue and empty, except for three clouds shaped like muffins. I had less than an hour to find Tante Amélie's office. I unfolded the map of Toronto and looked for the university. I had worried that it would take me hours to get to my aunt's office, but I realized the campus was not far away. I still didn't have time to lose.

The smell of frying onions and barbecued sausages made me realize that I was hungry. Despite the fact that my St. Mary's English vocabulary had abandoned me, I soon found that it is possible to negotiate the purchase of a hot dog by lots of pointing and smiling. As I was loading the hot dog up with sauerkraut, mustard, relish, and ketchup, my cell phone rang. It was Maman. I ducked into a lane between two buildings to answer it.

"*Bonjour, chérie,* how are you? What's that noise? I thought I heard an ambulance siren."

"I'm fine. It's outside." *That much was true, at least.*

"What are you doing?"

"I . . . I'm eating an early dinner." *Also true.* "What about you?"

"Madame Tremblay is asleep, so I grabbed the phone and called you, *chérie.*"

I gulped down the whole hot dog while she told me about the old lady, who seemed cheerful enough, despite confusing my mother with her own daughter. I didn't want to leave the lane because I was afraid that Maman would hear telltale big-city sounds, but I was desperate to get her off the phone.

"Let me tell you about the islands," she said. "They are so lovely! I haven't seen the ocean yet, but the air is fresh, and I can smell the sea. The people are nice. What will you do tonight?"

I stepped back onto the sidewalk and started toward the university.

"I'll probably watch TV. And you?"

"Well, it depends on Madame Tremblay. Her daughter is coming over tonight."

I tried to speak, but I was drowned out by a bike courier's bell.

"I can't hear you! What's the noise in the background?"

A man with a sandwich board walked by, yelling what sounded like a warning that the world was ending.

"The TV."

"Turn it down, or you'll go deaf. And you don't want the neighbors to think you're running wild. I'll call you tomorrow. Sleep well."

"*Oui, Maman.*"

"And don't forget to take your whistle with you wherever you go, okay?"

I stepped off the curb to make way for a woman with three small white dogs on jeweled leashes. "*Oui, Maman.*"

"And don't forget to lock the door when you go to bed, OKAY?"

"*Oui, d'accord.*"

"Good. Have a good night. *T'es toujours mon bébé.* I love you."

"Yes, I know. *Je t'aime aussi.*"

I could tell that she was trying her best not to cry, but her voice betrayed her. I could feel her loneliness, and that just made me want to end the conversation as fast as I could. I hated myself for that and for lying. It was getting all too easy. I started to run, the pack bouncing against my back.

Bloor Street was teeming with people, all of them hurrying. The women looked impossibly well groomed, in high-heeled shoes that made them look as if they were walking into a head-wind. I huffed past big new magazine-land stores: Hermès Paris, Cartier, Tiffany & Co. At GUESS, I stopped to catch my breath. The windows reflected a sweaty, plump, unkempt girl with hair like straw, who looked older than seventeen, with a flowery pink backpack, standing on a chic street hundreds of miles from home.

"Change, please?" A boy around my age sat cross-legged on the sidewalk, with a Styrofoam cup in front of him and a hand-lettered sign that read I'M HUNGRY. I gave him the change from my hot dog – Karma – and he thanked me. *Had he set out with his own dreams?* I couldn't bear to think about that.

The stores glimmered, as if they were the ones alive and breathing and the people on the street there to serve them. I passed the Royal Ontario Museum with its weird architecture – it looked as if a big iceberg had crashed into the side of the building. I consulted my map and the piece of paper with Tante Amélie's address on it. St. George Street. I figured that the Department of Astronomy and Astrophysics was another ten minutes away. It was almost six o'clock.

A security guard sat outside the building on what looked like a lump of concrete, but what might have been a sculpture. He was peeling an orange. I fished out my cell phone and dialed Tante Amélie's number. I listened to her message again and noticed that, despite having lived in Toronto for over twenty years, she still had the trace of a French accent.

Please, leave your message after the tone. Tanks.

The thought of leaving a message she could erase terrified me. The enormity of what I'd done hit me, and I felt rooted to the ground. I'm sure I'd still be standing there if the security guard hadn't asked, "Looking for somebody? I'll be locking up in a few minutes." He spoke English with more difficulty than me.

"Professor Morissette." I sounded abrupt, though I was grateful. But I was afraid to try to frame a whole sentence, in case he didn't understand me.

"You're in luck. She's still in her office."

MIMI, THE NIECE

On the door to Tante Amélie's office was a plaque stating her name, a photocopied listing of her office hours, a snapshot of a cat, and a handmade sign that read PLEASE, KNOCK ON THE DOOR. DO NOT DROP IN AS IF YOU WERE A METEORITE. I knocked.

"Hello, what can I do for you?" Tante Amélie sat at a computer and hardly raised her eyes. Her thick black hair had shed a light dusting of dandruff on her black shirt. She looked a bit like Maman's cheery good-luck bingo troll.

"Can I help you?" she repeated.

"Do you recognize me?"

She looked at me as if I had three heads, with a flowerpot on each of them.

I tried again. "Do you know who I am?"

"Sorry, but it's been a very long time since I stopped playing guessing games. I've had more than ten thousand students since I started teaching, and I don't have all afternoon, so I would be really appreciative if you'd just tell me why you are standing at my door."

"It's me! *C'est moi* – Mimi Morissette. Marie's daughter. Your niece!" I said, with what I hoped was an endearing smile.

She didn't smile back. She just waved in the direction of the three chairs side by side in her office. Neat bookshelves lined the walls. There

64

were three published articles framed on the wall beside her diplomas, a picture of her shaking hands with Stephen Hawking, and another with astronauts Marc Garneau and Julie Payette.

Once I was seated, my knapsack at my feet, she finally spoke. "Well, I see that you've grown a lot. You were what, five, when I last saw you?"

She drew out the word "grown." That was an understatement. *Surprise, Tante Amélie! Your niece grew up into a beluga in a minimizer bra and a sweater looped around her butt to hide her fat because when you're as overweight as I am, despite your three thousand pounds and the fact that you look like a hippopotamus, you often feel invisible, undetectable, forgotten* – and that's what I felt most of the time.

"What a surprise!" she said, looking as if a bulldozer had just flattened her. "And what brings you to Toronto?"

"Sperm."

"Pardon?"

"I want to find out about my father. Meet him, maybe."

"I don't understand."

"All I know about my father is that he was a sperm donor in Toronto and –"

"Thank you for coming by. If you call me, I'll take you out for lunch while you're in town. I'm under the gun with this article, and I have to get to work." She turned back to her computer screen.

"Tante Amélie," I said.

"Yes?" She looked surprised to see me.

I was desperate. "Can I stay with you?"

"Unfortunately, I don't think that would be a good idea."

I know. Lying is bad and horrible and nasty, but I was beginning to panic. I didn't have a backup plan, and I didn't have the money to pay for a hotel room. Seeing that boy living on the street scared me. I didn't want to sleep between a parking meter and a fire hydrant. I blurted out the first thing I could think of.

"Maman has this dreadful sickness, and the doctors think that she won't make it to Christmas."

That got Tante Amélie's attention. She burst into tears. "*Mon Dieu!* She . . . oh, no! I can't believe it! She's so young!"

"She's not that young." *Good going, Mimi. Add "callous" to "liar" on the personality profile.*

"Your maman was a very courageous woman, you know. She tried to raise you the best she could."

Tante Amélie was right. Maman and I had always joked that she was a two-in-one, like detergent and fabric softener, or shampoo plus conditioner. A mom plus a dad. I felt sick at the thought of losing her.

"*Mon Dieu!* I can't believe it! I can't believe that

I used the past tense to talk about Marie. She's not dead yet! Sorry, sorry, sorry." She drew in long, painful gulps of air. "I need to talk to her. If she . . . I mean, if she goes before I have a chance to talk to her for a last time, I would . . . mon Dieu, I couldn't live with myself."

I wanted the clock to stop. I needed to think fast. "Well, maybe tomorrow? Maman is probably sleeping right now."

"You're right. I will call her tomorrow."

Tante Amélie covered her mouth with her hand and sobbed. She took off her glasses and laid them on the desk in front of her. She stood up and went to the window. From my vantage point, all I could see was her back. After a minute or two, she turned to me. "Of course you can stay with me," she said softly. "You can stay as long as you need to."

I felt like the world's biggest rat, but I had no idea whatsoever of how to undo what I had said.

"Let me call Professor Craig. He's the department head. This is such terrible news. I was supposed to see graduate students tonight. I want to go home. When did she find out she was sick?"

"A year ago." I was on a roll. "She tried all kinds of stuff, like chemotherapy and radiation. The doctors said there was nothing left to do but pray that she won't suffer too much."

I was getting better and better at this lying thing. I could make up anything. I didn't have to be Mimi anymore. All I needed was a story to tell. Pinocchio seemed like an amateurish little brat compared to me. *Did I feel guilty about my lies?* Sure, but I was possessed.

♡

I trotted to keep up with Tante Amélie's long, purposeful stride. She lived not far from her office, in an ornate Victorian house encrusted with verandas, balconies, and a turret, on a street lined with chestnut trees. There were three native dream catchers hanging in the front window and three balls of green wool stacked on the seat of a blue wooden rocking chair on the broad front veranda. When Tante Amélie opened the heavy oak door, I thought for a moment that I was back at St. Mary's. The walls were painted white, the wooden floors were gleaming, and a collection of books as big as the one at school lined the living room.

I took off my shoes and followed Tante Amélie to the kitchen, which ran across the back of the house.

"I don't drink pop or soda, but I have grape juice, tea, and water. Would you like something to drink? Don't mind the mess." She opened the refrigerator door and pulled out the ice tray.

"Water is fine, *merci*."

Her place was not a mess – far from it. I wondered if the clean gene was inherited. She certainly seemed as orderly as Maman. A water dish and a small bowl of kibble sat on a plastic mat with KITTY IS KING written on it.

"Why didn't you call me to tell me you were coming? Why didn't your mother call me?"

I was stumped for a moment. "A friend of Maman's has taken her to the mountains to rest."

Tante Amélie looked at me sharply. "Does she know where you are?"

"Sure she does. She just knew somehow that you'd take care of me." A professor is supposed to be smart, but Tante Amélie bought this without further comment. *Where had lying been all my life?*

"How long do you expect be in Toronto?" she asked me.

"One week." As soon as I finished my water, she took the glass from me, washed it, dried it, and put it back on the shelf.

"Why don't you sit in the living room while I make up a bed for you upstairs?"

"Thank you. This is really nice –" I didn't have a chance to finish my sentence. She was already climbing the stairs, muttering to herself. She didn't seem angry, just confused.

I felt the lovely roughness of the bleached white cotton that covered the sofas. An orchid in a celadon-glazed pot nodded on a glass table. Her books were grouped by subject, in alphabetical order by author. The novels were arranged just so: Margaret Atwood was the first in line, followed by Pierre Berton, Roch Carrier, Leonard Cohen, Douglas Coupland, Robertson Davies, Timothy Findley, and on and on and on. There were three copies of each book – a hardcover, a largish paperback, and a mass-market copy. I reached for *The Handmaid's Tale* and jumped when I heard Tante Amélie's sharp voice.

"If you're going to take a book, you have to put it back *exactly* where you got it."

"I'll be careful."

"It's okay, it's okay, it's okay."

Tante Amélie had come downstairs again. I could hear water running in the kitchen and her careful movements as she worked. I hoped fervently that what she was working on was dinner. Despite the hot dog, I was starved. Finally she appeared in the doorway to the living room, wearing a cotton caftan. She was carrying a tea tray, which she set on the coffee table. On the tray was a china teapot, a crystal sugar bowl, and three delicate mismatched cups and saucers. The only things to eat, other than sugar cubes, were three Digestive biscuits.

Once she had handed me the cookies, she said, "Do you like to read?"

Her question thrilled me. Nobody other than Maman had ever asked me that. "I love reading!"

"Your favorites?" She poured the tea and handed me a cup.

I couldn't think of a thing to answer, so I started babbling. "I love biographies and books about the British monarchy. Princess Alexandra is my favorite. I loved Céline Dion's biography, and Lady Di's too. . . . Did you know that Lady Di's favorite rock band was Dire Straits and that Humphrey Bogart was her seventh cousin and that she called Camilla Parker-Bowles 'the rottweiler'?" I went on and on.

Tante Amélie looked stunned. "How interesting," she said, although even I could tell that it wasn't. What's more, the list was as much a fabrication as my doting father and my friendship with the queen. The truth is, I love to read poetry and history and all kinds of things. *So why did I pretend that all I read was junk?*

"I'm not actually familiar with books about the British monarchy. Please, tell me more about your mother." She clinked her silver spoon in the teacup, creating quite a little whirlpool.

"She's doing fine," I said.

Tante Amélie looked up in surprise. I had forgotten momentarily about the terminal disease I'd given poor Maman.

"For a woman who has cancer," I added quickly.

"Who's taking care of her?"

"Well, she's in the hospital right now, and that's why I came here because before, when she was home, I took care of her, and . . ." Apparently Maman had come back from the mountains in the last hour or so.

"*Ma pauvre Marie.* I just can't believe it. Is she as much of a clean freak as she used to be?" Tante Amélie laughed fondly.

I didn't get it. We were talking about her sister's cancer, and then, out of the blue, she asked about her housekeeping habits. Then it occurred to me that I wasn't exactly in a position to be judgmental.

"Sure, but you know when you have a terminal illness, I guess that, physically, you are less inclined to clean?"

I was blathering. I had no idea how I had gotten myself into this knot. From the minute I left home, I had done nothing but tell one stupid lie after another. I had made up utterly unnecessary, and obviously improbable, stories – Post-its, for heaven's sake – to tell two perfectly nice strangers, and I'd sent poor innocent Tante

Amélie into a tailspin, thinking that her only sister was dying. I was supposed to be on a quest for the truth about myself, and all I did was treat the truth like so much sand that I could shape into any kind of castle I wanted.

All I really wanted to do was start over. I wanted to ask Tante Amélie why she and Maman had lost contact. I could remember a time when we exchanged Christmas cards, and I would always draw a reindeer (my specialty) beside my name, and there had been an exchange of birthday envelopes. And then Tante Amélie was gone from our lives.

"Dear Marie. Our maman loved a clean house too. She died when Marie and I were still kids," she said, her eyes full of tears.

I felt like a creep. My stomach grumbled. I didn't want to watch Tante Amélie sniff, so I took another look around the living room. Apart from the bookshelves, the walls were bare. The only piece of art was a small painting above one of the sofas. It was signed Riopelle. I remember studying him in visual arts in grade nine.

"You must be very tired." It was a statement. "You should go to bed."

"Well, to tell you the truth" – as if I could – "that would be a good idea."

"Come with me. I'll show you the guest room."

I followed her up the stairs to a small bedroom. The walls were the same arctic white as the living room. The only furniture was a single bed, a pine dresser, a plain pine chair, and a small wooden desk. The initials AM were carved into a corner of the desk. Perhaps it had belonged to her when she was a kid.

Tante Amélie didn't offer to help me hang up my clothes, or kiss me, or even say good night. She just closed the door very softly. I could hear her steps echoing on the wooden stairs.

I pulled open one of the dresser drawers. In it were neatly folded clothes, separated by sheets of tissue paper. I unwrapped a soft yellow bundle. It was a baby's sweater. The drawer was full of baby sleepers, soft dresses with little round collars, and a pair of white baby shoes with bells on the toes.

Why would Tante Amélie have a supply of things for a baby? I wondered. Babies were a subject I hated to think about at the best of times. In grade three, we were all handed a book entitled *How Babies Are Made*. The teacher drew a man and a woman together on the blackboard, with a big heart around them, and said, "When a man and a woman love each other very much, they can decide to have a baby." When I raised my hand and explained to her what my mother did to get pregnant, I saw the teacher's face turn from a soft pink to a burning Santa Claus red. After class, she gathered up the books, and we never saw them again.

I didn't try the other drawers. I left my clothes in my knapsack.

Before I got into bed, I heard a pigeon cooing dreamily at my window. I put the photo of Maman on my night table, pressed different pressure points on my left foot to try to kill my appetite, and swiped my toes with pink nail polish – the perfect cure for homesickness.

Chapter Seven

I lay in bed, so tired that my legs kept twitching, and listened to the unfamiliar night sounds of the house. I settled in for a visit with Céline.

Céline and the Cell Phone

I am sitting alone at a table in the school cafeteria, waiting to be attacked by flying food. This morning, Mrs. Maurice, aka The Giraffe, handed out the roles for the school play. Macy is going to star, of course. I am going to be a shrub. Princess Macy arrives with her entourage. Her legs are as slim as HB pencils. She sees me sitting by myself and whispers something to Akila. They both laugh. I try to ignore them as I eat my plastic container full of the lasagna I brought from home. Later, I am going to eat my choco-late bar in a cubicle in the washroom, so no one can say, "The fatty is eating lots of fat, and that's why she's XXL."

A cold wind blows across the cafeteria, and a light comes through the doors. It sparkles like a mirror ball. Then, a thin silhouette emerges, but I can't see it properly. It's all blurry. I try to look at it again, but it is way too shiny, too bright. The light is blinding. Then, I hear the music.

"I want to talk to Mimi, please. Where is she?"
The silhouette is calling my name.

"Mimi, ma belle, where are you?" says the voice, in English with a French accent as thick as mine. "Mimi, I've been looking for you! I have a gift for you — my official handbag, my official slippers, plus an official X-small pink T-shirt from my show in Las Vegas."

Yes. It is her, and she is talking to me. Not to Macy. Not to Akila. Me. She comes toward me with her microphone and asks if she can eat some of my lasagna. "It reminds me of my mother's cooking," she says.

"Oh, yes, yes, have it all if you want." Céline digs in with a happy sigh.

Suddenly she is solemn. Her smile disappears and she furrows her eyebrows the way she does when she sings "My Heart Will Go On," and, for some reason, she hands me her golden cell phone.

"Mimi, the call is for you," says Céline.

As I take the phone, someone touches my elbow.

♡

"Mimi, wake up! Your cell phone is ringing." Tante Amélie sounded concerned. She backed out of the room.

"Oui. Allô?" I said, half-awake.

"Chérie, how are you?"

"Sorry, Maman, I was sleeping. . . ."

77

"Well, I was worried about you. Are you okay? I heard the news."

What news? What news? I tried to think. "Everything is great, here, Maman, don't worry about me. . . ."

"You weren't afraid? I'm proud of you. How did you cope?"

Cope with what? I figured I'd better go on the attack. "Maman, I'm not six years old anymore. Stop treating me like a baby, okay?"

"You'll always be my baby, *chérie*, even when you get married and have children of your own. And a power outage can rattle anyone."

At last, a clue! A power outage. "I was fine. I found batteries for the flashlight and I just went to bed." *Good recovery, Mimi.* After I mollified Maman, I fell asleep again.

Tante Amélie knocked on the door. "Sorry if I woke you up, but I thought the call might be important, what with your mother in hospital," she said. In her blue pajamas, and with her hair in a ponytail, she looked like a frightened child.

"Thank you, it was just a friend."

Tante Amélie stayed in the doorway. I noticed that she was holding a card in her hand. I could see a big red heart drawn on it. I felt a lurch of recognition as I remembered the words.

My nose bled all over my Lego dinosaurs
thinking about you, Tante Amélie. Happy
Valentine Day!
XOXOXO
Mimi

"You kept that for all these years?" I said.

"Yes, I did." For the first time since I'd arrived, she smiled.

"Tante Amélie?"

"*Oui.*"

"Thank you for everything. I wish we could have spent more time together, you know." I hoped I had opened the door for another smile, or even a hug. Apparently not.

"I have to go to my office tomorrow morning, so I'll leave around eight. You can sleep in if you want. I'll put a key on the kitchen table for you."

"*Merci.*"

"*Bonne nuit,*" she said, closing the door. I unwrapped two squares of chocolate and tried to imagine myself in the guest bedroom at Buckingham Palace. The queen would come in and sit on the moiré love seat in the big bow window so that we could talk over the day while we sipped hot chocolate from china cups painted with butterflies.

♡

I woke up around nine to the rusty smell of rain on pavement. The cats gave me baleful looks as I found the key and read the note Tante Amélie had left on the kitchen table, anchored by a big jar of vitamins.

> There's food in the fridge. Help
> yourself. You already have my office
> phone number. Please, call only if
> there's an emergency. I have three
> cats in the house. Don't let them
> outside. They don't like visitors.
> Be careful.

What a welcome note. I could still smell coffee in the kitchen, but there was none left. I opened the fridge and saw apples and broccoli and asparagus. Eggs. Skim milk. No cheese. No meat. Not even a tiny bit of strawberry jam. Something furry streaked by and hid under a sofa in the living room. I hoped it was one of the cats.

I opened the kitchen cupboard. I wanted something good and solid, like muffins or bread and butter. Food that was comforting and calming. Qualities that were in short supply inside me. Today was the day when I might be solving the mystery of my life. I was frightened.

There was nothing remotely starchy in the

cupboard except a box of unsweetened granola. I poured a bowl for myself to take back to bed. Last night, I hadn't noticed the photographs that lined the staircase: Tante Amélie with a good-looking man, having a picnic in a park; a photo of Amélie, wearing a black robe and a mortarboard, shaking the hand of an old white-bearded man; a photo of her cats, playing with a ball of wool; Amélie and Maman in black minidresses, their eyes rimmed with liner and what looked like false eyelashes; a photo of a baby, sleeping in my aunt's arms. It was not me.

I spread my map on the bed and found the location of the sperm bank. I could walk. I took a shower and fished a clean T-shirt out of my knapsack. I thought I would feel a sense of occasion when I got this close to solving my mystery, but all I felt was numb. I set out.

The rain hadn't cooled the air. It was humid and hot. I turned on my iPod and listened to "A New Day Has Come," waiting for its magic to hit me. It didn't. I stared at every man I passed. Men in jogging shorts, men in ragged jeans, men in chinos. *Could any of them be my father?* Anything was possible. *Had my father walked this very street, where cicadas screeched overhead?*

Soon I was sweating, but I forced myself to put one foot in front of the other. *The next time I walk this block,* I thought, *I'll know who I am. I may have brothers and sisters. I will not be floating like a blimp, un-anchored and alone.*

Finally, I was almost there. My T-shirt was plastered to my back and my hair was frizzing up around my face. I wanted to look presentable and as unflaky as possible when I got to the sperm bank, so I stepped out of the shimmering heat into a coffee shop to cool off. I ordered a cappuccino milk shake. Its sticky sweetness, normally such an old reliable friend, made me sick. I couldn't finish it. Nor could I stand another moment of the longing inside me.

I counted the numbers on the buildings. The office should have been in the next block. It wasn't. All I could see was hoarding, studded with signs warning that no signs would be permitted. Behind the hoarding, I could hear the crunch and roar of construction equipment.

MIMI AND APOLLO

I had passed a bookstore with a coffee shop on the ground floor and I turned back to it. I bought another milk shake and rifled through magazines off the rack. I wanted to die. I did the next easiest thing. I opened a copy of *Majesty*. I would soothe myself with news about what the royals were up to at Balmoral this summer. *How was the salmon fishing?* I sat on the floor, my back against a bookshelf in the history section of the store, and prepared to visit the royal family.

That's when I saw him. Apollo. A Greek god. Beautiful wavy blond hair, bright blue eyes, and a charming, sweet smile that would melt any heart. He wore a black T-shirt. On it was pinned a badge with the name of the bookstore and his name, Luc. He was coming toward me. It looked like he was going to speak to me. I froze.

"Sorry, miss."

He *was* talking to me. He was actually talking to me, and I didn't think he was going to make fun of me. He had nice hands.

"Sorry to bother you, but you can't sit on the floor." He sounded like he was from Québec, but I was afraid to ask.

He pursed his beautiful lips.

"Oh! Sorry, so sorry!" I hauled myself up.

"No, I'm the one who's sorry. I hate to tell customers they can't sit on the floor, but if I don't, and my manager sees you, I'm in big trouble. . . ."

He came back with a chair. "That's for you, miss."

I tried desperately to think of something witty and gracious and adorable to say in English, or in French for that matter. I failed. I had to settle for thank you.

"No problem. Are you done with those magazines?" he said.

"Not yet," I said. "I'm Mimi, by the way."

"My name's Luc. I like your T-shirt. I have a big poster of that painting in my apartment." My T-shirt was green, with a print of Monet's *Water Lilies* across the front.

"Oh, really?" *Scintillating, Mimi. What a conversationalist.*

"Are you from Québec?"

"Yes. I'm trying to cope with English here. My accent is awful."

"Oh, but your English is pretty good. Please, don't get me wrong. . . ."

"Really?" At last, a reward for all those years at St. Mary's.

"I come from Québec too," he said, with a grin.

We played the kind of geography that people fall into when they are far away from home – what city, what neighborhood, what street. I told him I was from Rosemont in Montréal.

"*Bravo!*" he said.

I didn't know what was so great about coming from Rosemont. Our apartment was on a busy street that shook with the constant passing of delivery trucks. It was a world away from the leafy, quiet Annex where my aunt was living.

"I miss Montréal so much!" He looked like a puppy. I wanted to pat his lovely head.

"Me, too!" I didn't actually miss Montréal at all. I'd never lived in a place as nice as Tante

Amélie's, and I thought Toronto was exciting. But I would have said that I loved nailing my head to the floor if it meant having something in common with the gorgeous creature standing in front of me.

"Why don't we have a coffee? I'm finished at twelve. Are you free after that, say twelve-fifteen?" It sounded to me like he was asking for a date. All I could do was gawp like a fish.

I pinched myself to make sure I was not dreaming. This was better than anything I'd ever made up – beauty crowns, royal crowns, or Céline. Then a devil possessed me and made me say, "Twelve-fifteen? I don't know if I can make it."

Stupid, stupid, stupid. But suddenly, I was scared. *This guy can have all the girls he wants, why me? What's wrong with him? He must be an ax murderer or some kind of weirdo.*

Luc looked at the floor, and his smile disappeared. I couldn't stand it.

"Wait a second. You said twelve-fifteen, right? Listen, I'll make a phone call, and I'll try my best to be there, okay?"

"*Oui, d'accord!* So, see you at the front desk at twelve-fifteen, then?"

"Sounds perfect." I was grinning so hard, I must have looked demented.

♡

What a great city Toronto was! No father and no doting Tante Amélie yet, but I was so happy that I wanted to sing. I thanked every possible deity for the lovely people who had designed and made and sold the Monet T-shirt I was wearing. I sat back in the chair that Luc had brought me, reading free magazines and waiting for the first real date of my life. How I wished Akila and Macy were here to see me.

Along with the happiness came a big, unavoidable current of fear. *What if he just wants to laugh at me?* Maybe he was Macy's friend and just wanted to see how much fun he could have by teasing the Big Beluga. I had no idea why a hottie like Luc would want to have coffee with me. Surely it would take more than a T-shirt to turn me into date-worthy material.

It was hard to concentrate on the magazine interview with the man who trains the queen's corgis, but eventually it was time to meet Luc. I put the magazines back on the rack and walked to the front desk.

"Hey! Hi!" It was him.

"*Ça va?* How's it goin'?" I said, trying to sound cool.

"Are you hungry?" he said.

I was starving, but I would have died before I admitted it. I had learned from miserable experience to save my eating for private. (*Gee, you eat a lot!*

No wonder you're fat. Gee, you eat so little! How come you're so fat?) I wasn't about to take such a risk with Luc.

"No, but you can eat and I'll have a coffee."

"Awesome!" he said.

Even if he seemed to punctuate everything he said with an exclamation point, it didn't diminish the magic of the moment. *A date. A real date.*

We went to a restaurant that looked like a fake diner, with a sham jukebox and booths with red vinyl seats. Under all the trappings, it was just a fast-food burger place. I waited at a table (the seats were bolted to the floor, lest anyone feel the urge to steal one) while Luc placed the order.

As he unwrapped his hamburger and French fries, I studied his face. His eyes looked like Bambi's, I decided, with their fringe of dark eyelashes a startling contrast to his blond hair. I took a sip of my coffee. I didn't care that it tasted like battery acid. It was filling and it made me feel grown up.

"So, you come from Montréal," I said. A whiz of an opener.

"*Oui.* I'm studying history at the University of Toronto. I'm going into my second year."

"I love history!" I didn't mean to seem as enthusiastic as if he had just offered me a million dollars, but I did. *Oh, make me shut up.* I sounded like I was channeling Macy or Akila cooing over a pair of Manolo Blahniks. That was enough to snap me out of it. "I like British history," I said, like a normal person expressing an opinion.

"Why British?" He looked at me as if I had said that I enjoyed talking to windowsills as a hobby.

"I like to read about the kings and queens. I like the stories." *Lame, lame, lame!*

"Don't you think that the monarchy is anachronistic?"

"Well, don't you think that the whole point of monarchy is to be anachronistic?" I said. "I think that monarchy is supposed to keep the past alive when everything else is changing. I think it's important to know where we come from." I was quite pleased with myself.

"In the first place, we don't come from the British monarchy. We're Québécois. In the second place, it's not roots that count. I think everybody should be judged by what they do, not by who their ancestors are."

I tried my best to think of a way to defend the queen. I just loved the idea of her life. It seemed so graceful, set in lovely gardens, with her handsome husband and her sleek horses and the careful order of her days. And all her ancestors, with their well-known stories. She could go back a thousand years and know who her ancestors are. When I was little, I used make myself paper crowns to wear.

"I guess I just like glitter. The queen's life seems so . . . so shiny. Like Céline Dion's."

"I know what you mean. I love Céline Dion too."

Ooh-la-la! This was perfect. A hottie who was eager to ask a "chubbette" for coffee and who also loved Céline Dion. I had hit the jackpot.

"I dressed like Céline in the Pride Parade. Do you want some of my fries?" he said, rattling the paper cup of poutine.

Gay.

"I hope you're okay with that," he said, watching me.

"Are you kidding? I just love gay people!" I said enthusiastically, even though the only gay person I had ever met was Mr. McTavish at St. Mary's.

Luc snorted and his cola made him choke. He laughed.

"You know what? I think I'll have one of your fries, if that's okay with you." I reached across the table companionably. I should have felt worse. The clue to my father was a hole in the ground, and my first (and possibly last) date was with a gay guy who was homesick for a Montrealer. But I felt fine. No need to retreat to Balmoral or Las Vegas. Sitting in a faux diner on a hot summer day with a sweet guy was good enough for me.

As I dunked my French fry into ketchup (perfection – thick cut with the skin left on), I watched Luc to see if he was watching me stuff myself. He didn't seem to care.

We chewed in silence for a few minutes. A heavily studded waiter with a water jug paused at our table and gave Luc a smile that lasted just a moment too long. Luc blushed.

"Don't you mind that, Luc?" I asked.

"Not really. It's sure better than high school. The only time anybody paid any attention to me there was to make fun of me."

"For being gay? That's awful."

"We lived in a pretty rough area, and you weren't supposed to love books, so I was teased. I didn't even know I was gay until we watched a video in sex ed class. Two guys were walking along a beach holding hands. The teacher had to turn it off because the kids were yelling stuff like 'fags, fairies, pansies, fruits!' I was stunned. I said to myself, *That's me. I'm gay.* I didn't tell anybody.

"I knew I wasn't like this guy who'd been in my class since kindergarten. When we were little, he was always singing the Smurf song and picking flowers in the school yard. I hated going over to his house because all he ever wanted to do was play with his sister's dolls. By the time we got to high school, people yelled, 'Hey, whatzup, homo!' at him in the cafeteria. The teachers didn't do a thing about it. One morning, before the bell rang, he opened his locker. It had been vandalized with stuff like 'Fags = Satan' and 'Die in hell, faggot!' I remember the look on his face and how his hands were shaking. I never saw him again, not in school and not around the neighborhood."

"When did you come out?"

"I haven't told my brother, or my mother, or any of my macho uncles. I'm not ready. But Mathieu's folks know about him." He tore off a chunk of hamburger bun.

"Is Mathieu your partner?"

"Yes. One of the reasons I'm not out at home is because of what happened to him. He was talking on the phone with some guy he met on the Internet. His mother was listening on the line, and she started screaming at him. He found her crouched on the kitchen floor, throwing up. He didn't know what to do. He tried to hug her, but she said, 'Don't ever touch me again, you fag!' It was the last time he saw her. That was more than a year ago."

"Did you ever have a girlfriend?" I didn't want to sound like part of the Spanish Inquisition, but I felt drunk on the sense of being with a kindred spirit. Besides, I was curious.

"One. Maude. We liked the same kinds of books and movies. She flirted with me, and we started dating. I was in grade twelve, and, to be honest with you, I needed someone to take to the prom. When you go alone, people think that you're a loser."

No kidding, Luc. He must have guessed what I was thinking because he blushed. I patted his hand to let him know there were no hard feelings. I admitted that I was on intimate terms with the *make-up-a-boyfriend-who-lives-far-away-like-Saskatoon* syndrome and its major symptom, *the-picture-you-show-everybody-of-the-boy-who's-really-your-cousin.* I wondered if he had built up fantasy worlds as elaborate as mine, but we drifted away from the subject.

MIMI FALLS OFF THE WAGON

"I think I'm going to order a hamburger after all, with onion rings." I had to get away from the table to collect myself. Suddenly, I was ravenous. I stood in line at the counter. A tiny Asian woman ahead of me stepped aside to wait for her food while I placed my order. She nodded encouragement as I struggled to pronounce the words in English.

"It make you fat fat, Québec girl," she said, treating me to a brilliant smile.

"I guess," I said, looking at the blackboard displaying the menu, which hung above her head. I wanted to die.

I knew she was being impossibly rude, but her words still hurt me. They hurt like mad. What puzzled me was why I cared. I didn't know her and I didn't want to know her. She was nasty and she was nosy. Here I was on what I thought was my first date, even though the illusion had lasted only for a millisecond. Besides, apart from my unfortunate addiction to lying, I was a really nice person. *Why in the world was I giving some twerp power over me and what I felt?* Now that's neurotic.

By the time I got back to the table, Luc was absorbed in a book. I was tempted to say I'd read it too, but for the moment I'd lost my appetite for lying. "Is it any good?"

"*Mm.*" He used a scrap of napkin to mark his place and closed the book. "What are you doing in Toronto? Are you studying something?"

I may not have many social graces, but something told me that talking about my search for my sperm donor wasn't a topic for a first conversation. "Not exactly. I needed a break, you know." I hate when people say "you know" at the end of their sentences. *What could I expect him to know?*

"A break from what?"

"From school, from lots of things." I looked at the passersby outside the window.

"Cool!" he said, even though there was nothing cool in what I had just said. I probably wasn't ever going to see Luc again. I might as well find out what it feels like to be honest.

"I didn't exactly need a break from school. That's not true." I took a breath and studied my nail polish. It was smooth and unchipped, for once. "I'm here because I want to find my father."

"Why?"

I knew why. I used to watch *Sesame Street* every day and pretend that Big Bird was my dad. But a bird doesn't really count as a father figure. Over the years, I'd refined my vision of my fantasy father. He would fly into my life and sweep me away to a place where everything ugly and coarse and mean was banished. He'd love me, and it wouldn't just be me and Maman anymore. He'd have a good job so Maman wouldn't have to work so hard. He would like music and books and he would be interested in the kinds of history I like. We'd set up a chessboard and map out famous military campaigns together, and he would never laugh at me. . . .

When I didn't answer, Luc asked gently, "Did he leave you and your mother?"

"Not exactly. He was never actually with my mother. My mom went to a sperm bank."

Luc didn't blink. "But why are you in Toronto?"

"She got pregnant here. I know his sperm donor ID. That's the only thing I know about him. My mother's a big-time executive and she has houses here and in Paris and in –"

"Why do you want to find him?" Luc interrupted.

Why? For lots of reasons. One of them was the memory of Miss Shantz, my grade-two teacher. One day she handed out sheets of red construction paper and lengths of satin and lace ribbon. I couldn't wait. I'd never seen art supplies so lavish. Then she explained that we were to make cards for Father's Day. I didn't know what to do. The only significant male I knew was my hamster, René. I ended up making my Father's Day card for a rodent.

I answered carefully, testing each word as if it were a strange new taste. "I need to know where I come from. It would also be nice to know about his genetic background, like if he has cancer, or heart disease, or Alzheimer's, in his family. It's always useful to know." That's what I said, but deep down, that's not what I was looking for. I wanted to find my roots. If I knew him, perhaps I would know myself better. I also wanted the love of a father.

"I've tried to find my dad too."

"Really?"

"Yes, but I know that's not going to happen."

"*Pourquoi?*"

"He's dead."

"Oh. I'm sorry."

"Yeah. That's what people always say. He died when I was five. I don't remember much about him, except sitting on the floor of the kitchen, playing with plastic margarine tubs while my mom and brother and dad played poker."

"Do you miss him?"

"*Ça dépend.* I don't even remember the sound of his voice."

"At least, you have pictures of him, right? You know who he was."

"Yes, but I'd give anything to talk to him again. I get along with François, my brother. He's always been a father figure to me. You'll think I'm weird." Luc's eyes were full of tears. "I used to take the subway in the morning and pretend that maybe the man sitting next to me was my father. I thought that the spirit of my dad might want to be physically close to me and that he would take on the appearance of a stranger, so he could be with me. That's why I always smile at strangers, in case it's him."

"I don't think that's weird at all," I said. "I do the same thing. When I'm in the subway, or when I walk down the street, and I see a man, there's always this thought that maybe it's him."

The more we talked, the more ashamed I was at having made up the stuff about Maman, the big-time executive, and all her houses. But I don't think Luc believed me, and I don't think he cared.

We talked until a waiter brushed the lunch specials off the blackboard and started printing the dinner menu.

Out on the sidewalk, Luc gave me a heart-breakingly beautiful smile and scribbled on a bookmark. "Look, here's my phone number. Call me." I watched as he walked away. The sky was blue and the air had grown fresh. I took a deep breath and started toward the Annex. Then I thought about the great big gut-busting plate of food I had devoured for lunch and my sense of happiness evaporated. I rifled through my aunt's bathroom cupboard and found a bottle of laxatives and poured a slug down my throat.

Chapter Eight

$\mathcal{B}$y the time Tante Amélie came home at six with a bag of groceries, the laxative had begun its work. I felt ready for a new start. I longed to tell her about everything that had happened that day, but I didn't know where to begin. We ate a silent dinner of take-out sushi and raspberries. "Don't let the cats out," Amélie called after me, as I stepped out onto the porch to use my phone.

This time I barely had to lie to Maman. In fact, I could hardly get a word in. She sounded so happy to be in beautiful surroundings. She went on and on about the peace and the birds and the way the sun glinted off the water.

I told her I loved her, and I let her go back to work. She'd been sitting in the garden, reading aloud to Madame Tremblay.

I went to find Tante Amélie. She was reading an article in the *Journal of Astronomy* in the living room. With one hand she turned the pages, licking her finger three times each time, and with the other hand she was petting Salome, her tabby, who lay stretched out beside her on the sofa.

"Could you stop doing that?" she said, without looking up.

I jumped. "What am I doing?"

"Humming."

"*Pardon.*"

She closed the journal and laid it carefully on the glass table. I felt like she was startled to see me sitting in her living room and had to remind herself who I was. "You must be bored."

I didn't know what to say. I wasn't bored, exactly. That would have been impossible in a house bursting with books. It's that I had such a strange feeling of being unsettled.

"Why don't you go on-line? Let me show you how."

I followed her up to the computer room and watched her log on.

"*Merci*, Tante Amélie. *Merci.*" She gave my head three tentative pats.

♡

It took less than a minute to get the information I wanted. I typed in "sperm bank Toronto" and found out, after checking my map, that I was a five-minute walk away from the new address. I wouldn't even have to take a streetcar or a bus or a subway to get there. The enormity of what the words on the screen meant was hard to absorb. I didn't know what to do. *Should I call them? E-mail them? Walk in?* I got into my e-mail account and I began to type.

♡

While I waited for a response, I doodled on the keyboard. I visited a beauty pageant site that was full of ads for coaches, waxing tips, and colloidal tips (*what are colloidal tips?*). I found out where to buy a wholesale tiara and how I could parlay a walk across the stage into a walk down the catwalk in Paris. I stared at a dress in mauve and debated whether it would look more flattering than the soft buttery yellow chiffon. I thought about what I would say when they asked me what my wish for the world would be, should I win the crown.

Minutes passed. Finally, *You've got mail.* The message said *undeliverable.* I felt a strange sensation, as if I had had a narrow escape.

MIMI'S MASTER PLAN
If I was going to find my sperm donor, I was going to need more time in Toronto than the week I'd planned. I went into battle-plan mode again, ticking off what I had to do. First, I called Denise and Fred to let them know that they would have to find their way back to Montréal

without me. After a great deal of reassurance, Denise mustered the courage to find Montréal on her own. I felt bad about letting them down.

Next, there was the question of supporting myself. I hadn't thought I'd be staying any longer than a week, so I didn't have enough money to pay for transportation, or to get back to Montréal, before Maman discovered I was not safely settled in front of "The Dr. Phil Show" in our apartment. I would have to get a job. That had never been a problem for me. Maybe because I'm sort of substantial looking, I am the kind of teenager who has "reliable" (if they only knew) stamped on her forehead. And I have had a series of jobs: I've poured coffee, cleaned the floors at the nursing home where Maman worked, and walked a cranky basset hound that lives in our building. But finding work in a strange city with my accented English was another story.

I phoned Luc. "I need a job. Do you have any ideas? I have only enough money to last me until the end of the week, and I can't mooch off Tante Amélie. I sure can't ask Maman to give me money." Then I remembered. "Even if she has enough money to buy everything I want," I added lamely.

Luc let that last part pass. "Why don't you work at the bookstore with me?"

"I can't do that. What if somebody asks me a question about a book?"

"That's what computers are for. My roommate, Fiona, works there too, and she told me they haven't replaced someone in her department who left for lunch one day and didn't come back. I guess it's hard to find somebody because everyone's either already got a summer job or is away."

I started to make excuses, but he cut me off. "Come by the store on Monday morning and talk to the manager. Her office is in the building next to the bookstore."

Check that off my list for the moment. Now came the biggest challenge. When I went back downstairs, Tante Amélie was brushing the cats in the little mudroom off the kitchen. Before I could say anything, she said, "How long are you planning to stay? I have a lot going on right now, and I need to know." The cats were on their backs around her, paws waving, obviously enjoying the attention. "Who's the sweetest kitty in the world? Who's the handsomest?" She sang little kitty tunes to them as she brushed first one and then the other.

"Would you mind if I stayed here longer?" I patted one of the cats, and it grabbed my hand in all four paws.

"Doesn't your mother need you?"

"She needs a break." That much was true. Then I caught myself. "She thinks I need a break."

"Without checking with me? Oh, well, I guess she's not feeling too much like worrying about the niceties. You can stay. . . ." She sounded reluctant.

I tried to thank her, but she wasn't listening. It was late, and I was starving.

"Do you mind if I go to the store?" Maman would never have let me go out this late, but all Tante Amélie said was "Go ahead," as if she couldn't understand why I bothered asking.

The rain was coming down in sheets, but I didn't care. I bought a tub of chocolate ice cream. When I got back, the big oak front door of Tante Amélie's house had swollen in the rain. I tugged with both hands. Finally it gave and, as I propped it open with my foot to pick up the bag with the ice cream, something gray streaked by me.

Bloated with chocolate ice cream and relief that I wouldn't be living on the street while I looked for my father, I fell onto my bed with an old *National Geographic* from the pile that was stored in a corner of my room. I must have dozed because Tante Amélie's cry made me jump. "Salome! Salome?"

I went downstairs. "What's wrong?"

"Salome's missing. The tabby."

Oh, no. I had let her out.

"Have you seen her?"

"*Non.*" This wasn't a fantasy lie. This was a huge, save-your-life lie. I felt sick.

I helped Amélie look around the house, under bushes, and under the cars parked along both sides of the street. I held my breath as we shone a flashlight up and down the road. No cat body.

♡

We spent the next day knocking on doors, asking if we could check backyards and garages. Except for disturbing a dozy skunk curled up under a veranda and two kids who were smoking in a tool-shed, we didn't turn up anything.

When we finally dragged ourselves home, sweaty and tired, we had a silent dinner of sliced tomatoes.

"It's my fault! I must have let her out." Amélie said, crumpling in my arms. She wept.

I have never, ever, felt such self-loathing.

Chapter Nine

The next morning, I woke up at six – just to make sure I would be ready for my interview. Amélie was already up, and hoarse from calling Salome's name. A pile of posters with Salome's photo and the word REWARD was stacked on the counter.

"What are you going to do today?" she said. She was so distracted and anxious that I could almost feel the electric jolts of worry shooting from her.

"I'm going for a job interview at the bookstore around the block. They need someone right away, so there's a chance that, if they hire me, I'll start today. After that, I may have dinner with a boy who works at the store." This would have been earth-shaking news to Maman, but Tante Amélie seemed to take in stride the notion of me as a normal teenage girl who would naturally have friends. "Can you use some help putting up the posters?" She gave me a grateful smile.

We set out with a staple gun, tape, and the pile of posters. We were attaching the last poster to the bulletin board at the convenience store when Amélie asked me if I'd like to bring my new friend to see the dome, where she charted the stars.

Surprise gave way to a wave of guilt so strong that it made me woozy. I was so ashamed of myself. I had descended on her. I had told her a colossal, hurtful lie about my mother, and I had lost her cat. I didn't know if I could stand her being kind to me. So I did what I always did. I escaped, this time into Beauty Pageant Land.

Mimi, the Beauty Queen

This is the morning of the big pageant. Reporters ask me for tips on a healthy breakfast. I explain that I will eat a banana, oatmeal sweetened with apple sauce, and I will drink a glass of water. I will prepare a turkey sandwich for lunch, with apple juice.

♡

Tante Amélie's voice pierced through the pink fog. "You must be worried beyond belief about your mother, and you've been so sweet helping me try to find Salome. I didn't even notice when she got out."

We walked home to change before I went for my interview and she went to the university library. Maybe it was the aftermath of all her tears, but Amélie was talkative and confiding.

"I . . . I sometimes have difficulty in interact-ing with people," she said. "I don't know if you noticed, but I have an obsessive-compulsive dis-order and, unfortunately, it makes me awkward. I'm not the kind of person who can just go up to people and say, *Cut me some slack! I'm obsessive-compulsive!* Even your mother doesn't know how bad it's become."

The more she talked, the more I felt like crying. *What kind of person was I?*

"I'm just so grateful that you're here. Things are terrible at work, and now, with Salome missing . . ."

She sniffed. Scum Girl didn't say anything.

"I hope you and your friend can come to my office tonight. I think you'd like it. What's his name?"

"Luc," I said.

"Luc. How about nine o'clock? If it's clear, we can open the dome and look at the stars. It's a *cool* place, as my students say."

"*Merci beaucoup*, Tante Amélie."

"Good luck today. I really mean it."

♡

I went upstairs to call Luc. It was his day off, but we agreed that if I got the job, we'd meet for dinner and then go to Tante Amélie's office when it started to get dark. I put on some lipstick, a fresh T-shirt under my best cotton sweater, and tied my hair back. On the way to the bookstore, I couldn't stop thinking about how difficult it would be to live like Tante Amélie. I was afraid of being teased and taunted, but there wasn't something inside me that forced me to repeat things, or turn in circles, or count out endless groups of three.

Mimi, the Crime Fighter

I filled in the bookstore office's elaborate application form, listing my meager credentials, and took it with me to Mrs. Pitt, the manager of the store. She was perched behind an ornate desk carved out of blond wood. Despite the books and catalogs that covered every flat surface and the cardboard boxes full of bookmarks and rolled posters, her office had an odd sense of coldness. Everything about Mrs. Pitt was stiff, from her blonde pageboy to her bright pink manicured nails and cakey makeup. She looked like a grown-up version of Macy, so naturally she scared me almost senseless. She nodded to me to sit down, flicked on her BlackBerry, and kept her eyes fixed on the tiny screen. "Mimi Morissette, is that correct? Do you speak French?"

She reached for my application. "You graduated with honors from St. Mary's?" Before I could answer, she continued as if reading from a script. "The person in this position should have a demonstrated enthusiasm and talent for working in a team-based retail environment. Are you that person?" She had obviously delivered this speech many, many times before.

"Yes, I am, ma'am," I said.

"The job requires an individual who is passionate about selling, has excellent communication skills, high energy, and a willingness to learn. They must achieve results. Are you that person?" she said, looking at me for the first time. She frowned. I think. Apart from the fact that she didn't deviate from her script, her face didn't register much of anything.

"Yes, I am."

"You speak French?" she asked again.

"Yes, ma'am."

"Excellent." That made her perk up. "Can you start today? You will be put on a day's trial. If you have what it takes, you're hired. By the way, there's a lot of up and down the stairs involved. Great aerobic exercise." She paused, as if I should be pleased. Then I caught on.

"You have such a pretty face" she said. What she was really saying was *such a pretty face attached to such an ugly body.*

My pleasure in the heavenly prospect of working surrounded by books just about evaporated as I sank back into my dumpy body. *Was Mrs. Pitt trying to be helpful or cruel? Or just accurate?*

After yet another dreary stint with the human resources officer, who handed me one form to sign after another, I was ready to start. Mrs. Pitt was at the door of the bookstore when the security guard checked me in. "*Ah*, Mimi! Ready for the day?" She didn't wait for me to answer. "Perfect! Here's Fiona. You will follow her everywhere she goes and do everything she does. For God's sake, what are you doing? The rain dance?"

I was shimmying out of my sweater. I had needed an X-large, but when I bought it, I had stuffed myself into the large and was too embarrassed to ask for a bigger size. Once I managed to squirm out of it, I tied the arms around my waist and I pinned the badge with MY NAME IS MIMI. CAN I HELP YOU? to my chest.

"Finished? Come, girls. Time to work."

Fiona was an Asian girl who had jet black hair in a ponytail, heavy black glasses, and clomping black shoes that made her twiglet legs look all the more fragile. Sweet and sour, that was Luc and Fiona. Luc was sweet and gentle. Fiona had, to say the least, an edge.

"Hey! How's it goin'?" she said. "Luc told me about you. You actually want to work here?"

"I want to try."

"Okay. It's your funeral. Here are the rules. First off, Pitt is a 'witch' with a 'b,' but as long as you treat her like the queen, and say yes, yes, yes, whenever she talks to you, you can do pretty much whatever you want."

"I don't think she's crazy about me."

"Why? Because she gave you the old Frozen Face? She's had so much Botox that it's impossible to read her expression, and she's had so many facelifts that her eyes don't blink on their own. She has to do it manually."

"Thanks," I said doubtfully. At least I knew that her lack of expression wasn't anything personal.

"You're welcome. If somebody had told me that on my first day, life would have been much easier. I would have been spared hours worrying that she was mad, when all she was was frozen. And don't look right at her teeth – they're so white and shiny, they can blind you. Notice how thin she is? Word has it that she had two ribs removed."

Fiona was funny, but her acid words worried me. If she was this vicious about a good-looking woman like Mrs. Pitt, whose only sin was trying to stave off old age, what in the world would she have to say about me?

All the time she was talking, she was leading me to the second floor. She showed me how to use the computer, so when people asked for a book, I'd know how to find it.

"Basically, you treat customers like kindergarten kids, except you call them sir or ma'am – especially those who are sitting on the floor and reading stuff, as if this were a library. You say, 'Sorry, are you done with those?' They say yes, and you pick them up and put them back. Wash your hands every chance you get. Some customers are just disgusting, I mean, they'll do things, like lick their index finger before they turn the pages, and what they do with their noses is just too gross to think about."

I spent the day following Fiona everywhere. Nothing seemed to faze her: not the sweet old man who asked, "I'm looking for a book. I can't remember the title or the author, but it's sort of green"; not the formidable woman carrying a handbag worth more than a month's rent for most people, who griped about the price of a gorgeous atlas; and not the beefy guy who complained to Fiona because he had guessed wrong about the killer in a murder mystery she'd recommended. She was unfailingly pleasant to everyone.

For the last hour of the day, Fiona left me alone to see how I would cope. I was straightening up the magazine racks while keeping an eye on a girl – no more than sixteen, with long red hair – who'd spent ages thumbing through every gossip rag on the shelves. Finally, she stood up, leaving everything scattered on the floor. Except for the big glossy magazine she stowed in her bag.

She was beautiful, a state that normally would have made me cower. But I needed this job. I wanted this job. I liked this job. So I asked myself, *What would Céline do?* and found myself saying, "Hey, you have to pay for that!"

"For what, tubby?" Happily, I didn't know what "tubby" meant, until I looked it up later. It wasn't part of the English vocabulary that Mrs. McKnight taught. But I did know that she was stealing.

"Pay for it, or I'll call security."

She pulled the magazine out of her tote, tearing the cover. "This? It's yours." She turned on her heel and marched to the escalator.

"Good for you!" It was Fiona. I have to say, I was proud of myself, even though the magazine was too crumpled to sell.

Fiona helped me pick up the rest of the magazines. "I hate these magazines," she said. "Look at this stuff: 'Six tricks for perfect lips.' How about 'your back-to-school body'? This is just a bunch of ads interrupted by pictures, and people are dumb enough to pay to have someone sell them stuff."

Fiona turned to an article on a pop singer/TV actress. "Oh, joy! She finally lost that pesky ten pounds and she can fit into her wedding dress. Now my life is complete."

I realized that I wouldn't be confiding my beauty-pageant fantasy to Fiona anytime soon.

♡

When five o'clock finally came and a new set of salespeople arrived for the evening shift, I went to see Mrs. Pitt. I couldn't tell if she was glad or not that I had passed muster. Her forehead was serene and her eyebrows were in a perpetual surprised arch as she told me that I could come back tomorrow morning, same time, same place.

Chapter Ten

"How did it go?" Luc asked, looking at himself in the bubbly mirror that covered one whole wall of the crowded Thai restaurant. He pulled his lips back to check his teeth.

"Great! My aunt asked if tonight you want to come and see the dome where she works. She's an astronomer." I opened the stained menu.

"*Bravo!* When I was little, I used to pretend that I was a sailor, charting my way by the stars." Luc laid his cell phone on the table. "Just in case Mathieu calls," he explained. "What do you think of Fiona?"

I didn't want to admit that she scared me. "I've never met anyone like her," I said. (That, at least, was true.) "Tell me about her."

Apparently Fiona was from Vancouver, where her father owned a grocery store. Luc met her in their women's study class, and they ended up moving out of residence and into an apartment together. Fiona's older brother was studying to be an engineer when he died three years ago in a car accident. Before he died, her brother signed his organ donor card. His liver and his heart and his corneas all went to different people. Since then, Fiona's parents spent most of their time trying to track down the people who had his organs. They just ignored Fiona.

"What a story," I said. It was certainly more interesting than anything I could have dreamed up, and besides, I liked Fiona.

"Everybody has a story, if you take the time to listen."

MIMI AND MARS

The first time I had seen Tante Amélie's office, I was so nervous about meeting her that I could have been on Mars and I wouldn't have noticed. Being there with Luc made me take stock. A dusty mini solar-system mobile hung from the ceiling, and one of the bookshelves was covered in photos of a little girl. Someone had painted a quotation on the wall: "I maintain that the cosmic religious feeling is the strongest and noblest motive for scientific research. Albert Einstein. 1954." On the facing wall hung a framed certificate: "Winner of the Royal Astronomical Society of Canada's Gold Medal." Next to it, another framed certificate stated that "Amélie Morissette has an honorary moon citizenship and mining rights to whatever minerals might eventually be found below the surface."

"Awesome! Is this real?" Luc asked. "Can you really be a citizen of the moon?"

"Yes. I own a 500-square-meter plot of lunar land," Tante Amélie explained. "I know. There's no air or water, the daytime high soars to 100°C and the nighttime low dips to -173°C, but I thought it would be fun to dream about a permanent colony on the moon, don't you think?"

"Awesome!" said Luc again. And it was. The idea truly filled me with a sense of awe. I thought how nice it would be to go and live there, a citizen of a pristine place without any history.

Tante Amélie chose a key from a bulging ring and unlocked a door that lead from her office to a vast room. We followed her in. By the window stood a huge telescope, its lens as big as my face.

Luc's cell phone rang. As he listened to the caller, his face turned white. "I'm sorry, I have to go," he said. He gave me a hurried kiss and shook Tante Amélie's hand good-bye.

"I hope everything's okay," I called after him, but he was already racing down the hall toward the elevator.

Once he was gone, Tante Amélie turned the knobs that opened the dome above us, and we could see the beautiful night sky. Even though we were right downtown, the sky was bright.

"If you look carefully, you can see hundreds of stars," she said. "Can you see the faint differ- ences in color? Some of them are white and some, bluish. Can you see the star above that tree? In a few minutes, it will be higher in the sky. In the beginning, there were absolutely no stars, no planets, no atoms or molecules, and no life. Isn't that unbelievable?" She moved over, so that I could look in the telescope. "Can you see anything?" she said.

"Why does everything wiggle?" I asked.

"It's turbulence in the air, like tiny bubbles that distort the image you see. A little bit like when you're looking far to the horizon on a very hot summer day. Do you know how many nights I spend here, between these walls, looking at the sky?"

The way she said it was not a question. It was more of an observation, an affirmation.

"Do you know what it means to own the key I have in my hand?" she said.

"Tell me," I replied.

"It's been hard for a woman in this depart- ment. We've come a long way. A very long way." She put the key ring back in her skirt pocket and looked at the sky: "Life appeared on at least one tiny planet with an average star, in a spiral galaxy called the Milky Way. On this very special planet, life-forms adapted with the ability to think and speak and wonder, *Did it happen only here?* Maybe it happened on other planets, in other galaxies, too. Did you know that Mercury has ice on its poles, and Mars and Saturn have moons? It seems reasonable to speculate that life is cosmically probable."

Tante Amélie was in her element. She seemed like a different person, a member of another species – no longer the sad individual who measured out her life at home in sets of three.

"How did you get interested in all of this?" I said.

She put her hands in her pockets, perched on her desk, and kept her eyes fixed on the night sky above. "I was about your age when I watched the spacecraft *Viking* landing on Mars. That was it. I was hooked. I was sitting in front of the TV, watching anxiously for a close-up of the surface of Mars."

"And?"

"No clear evidence of life. Only dry riverbeds, which indicated that Mars once had liquid water on its surface. A denser atmosphere may be sufficient to support life. But who knows?"

As she talked about Mars and the planets and asteroids and distant galaxies, I could see stars in her eyes, shining brightly.

"But why is it so important for you to know if there is life beyond Earth?"

Tante Amélie looked at the sky with wonder and delight, as if it were a gleaming diamond. "Mimi, you look so much like your mother – the same smile, the same laugh. . . ."

She hadn't answered my question. Instead, she touched me – she stroked my hair. Then she turned the twenty-five-tonne telescope with her fingertips and showed me how to close the dome. We turned off the lights, and she closed the door behind us.

Back in her office, she led me to an old sofa. She pointed to a framed picture of a child, a smiling little girl. No hair, just a scar on the right side of her pumpkin head. She looked about three years old and was wearing a white dress with two ribbons streaming down the front. She was dancing barefoot and grinning at the camera, her tiny silver earrings and bracelet glinting in the sunshine.

"Beautiful, wasn't she? She loved holding my middle finger and making circles with it on the tip of her nose." Tante Amélie closed her eyes. "Her name was Joséphine. She was such a character."

"Who was she? She had a balloon face," I said tactlessly, but Tante Amélie didn't seem to care.

"From chemotherapy. My daughter. *Ma p'tite fille.*"

"Maman never told me you had a daughter," I said.

She took another picture off the shelf and sat beside me. Tante Amélie was young in this one. She was cradling a small child in a rocking chair, in a dimly lit hospital room.

"You can't see it here, but there were four IV tubes dangling from the central line in her tiny chest. My baby was so sick. There was a machine blowing warmed oxygen in her face to help her breathe. Joséphine almost died that night. She murmured about wanting to go 'upstairs,' to be with the stars. I told her that it was okay to go, and, the next day, that's what she did."

Tante Amélie lowered her head to her knees and covered her face with her hands. I put my hand on her shoulder, and she took it and kissed it.

"*Pardon*, Mimi. I thought that the Grand Canyon had dried up, but apparently there is still some water left," she said, with a Kleenex crushed in her fist. "When Joséphine died, I knew, without a doubt, that she would be with the stars."

We could hear the *wah wah* of an ambulance siren on the street far below and a car's angry honking. Sounds carried on the warm night air.

"I was already an astronomer, but when Joséphine died, I guess my search to know if there is life beyond Earth comes from wanting to hear the sound of my child's voice. I kept waiting for the stars to send me a message. You know, the mind can be very kind to us. It helps us find ways to bear things that are unbearable. Our human desire to communicate is so deep and so strong that we are willing to send messages, although we're not sure who might receive them."

Tante Amélie's words vibrated inside me. I realized that I wanted to find my father not so much to know about him, but to let him know that I exist.

She touched the tip of my nose with her finger. "Despite all the nights I've spent here, watching the sky and the stars and the planets, I've never found her. But when I look into your eyes, I can imagine the way she would be, and I'm sure she'd be as beautiful as you are."

I wanted to hold on to every word. Tante Amélie had generously given me a glimpse of what it feels like to be accepted and treasured, and I guess that's what being beautiful is. There's a French expression, "*bien dans sa peau*," that describes a happy level of ease with oneself. I'd never given it much thought, but the words came back to me like the answer to a riddle I'd been asking all my life.

We walked home and, for the first time, one of her cats, which was lying in front of the fireplace between two piles of books, curled around my legs in welcome.

Chapter Eleven

$\mathcal{I}$ woke up at dawn the next morning, quaking about what would happen when Tante Amélie realized that she was harboring the World's Biggest Liar. The thought made me so hungry that I could have eaten everything in sight – the desk, the mattress, and the bed. I hate myself when I feel that hungry, and I have developed a raft of ways to distract myself. There's the pressure points in the foot gambit, but it didn't work. Then there's knitting. I have knitted enough scarves to deck out an army, but I had no wool or knitting needles. I wanted to call Luc to make sure he was okay, but it was far too early. So I dipped into the fantasy bank and came up with the queen.

The Queen's Picnic

The queen and I are tramping through the heather on the hills beyond Balmoral. We find a shady spot beside a clear dark stream and spread out a picnic lunch of fried chicken and potato salad, with lovely bits of olive and egg and celery.

♡

This didn't help the hunger, but it did pass the time. I could hear Tante Amélie on the porch calling, "Salome! Salome!"

When I came downstairs, waves of sadness seemed to emanate from Tante Amélie's tense body. The kitchen table was set for three. The two cats looked at me reproachfully from their perch on the counter. I was sure they had the goods on me.

"Do you like to read the newspapers?" she asked, pushing the sections she'd finished across the table.

"Sure," I said, spreading out the front section. I'm addicted to letters to the editor. I read the ones that sound wise and funny, and if they are written by a man – you guessed it – I imagine that he's my father.

"Mimi, can I tell you a secret? I love to read personal ads. Some of them would break your heart. It's amazing how short and sweet some can be. Nothing but age, gender, race, sexual orientation, height, size. The sum of a whole human being."

The idea of Tante Amélie poring over the personals was a stunning one. She took three sips of coffee and pressed her eyes with her fingertips. "Don't mind me. I didn't sleep very well. I woke up around three this morning, and I couldn't stop thinking about your maman. I have a favor to ask. The last thing I want to do is upset her, but I really want to speak to her. Could you ask your maman if I can call her? This quarrel has lasted far too long. Two sisters shouldn't act like this."

Oh, no. What in the world was I going to do? Was I going to have to kill off Maman? There didn't seem to be any other way to prevent Tante Amélie from finding out that Maman was alive and well, not to mention being furious. I needed time to think. "Sure. I'll call her tonight.

"Tante Amélie, let me help you with the dishes. Is there something wrong?" She had started to cry again, silently and painfully.

"It's everything. Your mother, of course, and things are falling apart at work. And this stupid obsessive-compulsive thing makes me so tired and fed up. I wish I could be normal, like everybody else. Who wants somebody as twisted as me? Even my cat ran away."

"I like you, Tante Amélie." As soon as I said it, I realized it was true.

"That's not the same thing. I'm scared to grow old alone. I was never a great beauty, but it's hard to see everything starting to droop." She let her shoulders sag and gave a rueful little snort.

"Maman says that we age according to how we live."

"How would she know?"

"She works with old people, and she says that even with the really wrinkly ones, she can tell whether they were mean or kind or generous. I mean, she used to work with old people, when she was well enough to work."

Tante Amélie didn't react. She dried her hands on the dishcloth. "I have to face it. I have gray roots. I have back fat. I suppose that if I wore high heels and clothes that I couldn't breathe in, I'd be a more marketable commodity. I'm going to be alone and die with my cats – they're the longest-running relationship of my life. Aren't you, guys?" She rattled a tin of cat cookies at them, and they mewed at her expectantly.

I had thought that Tante Amélie, with her awards and her great house and all, was above all this.

"Did something happen at work?" I asked.

She picked up one of the cats and cradled it. "I'm feeling particularly glum this morning. I just checked my e-mail, and the weasel who's the head of the department sent me a message that I got turned down for a research grant. He didn't have the nerve to tell me to my face. What's worse, a woman who's been with the department for only a year got it. I know it's not rational, but

I can't help thinking that she got it because she's younger than me." She straightened the pile of newspapers and then straightened it again. "Forgive me, Mimi. I shouldn't be unloading all my craziness on you. Chalk it up to too much time alone. I'll be okay once classes start again in the fall."

"I don't mind. You're talking to the world expert on not having anyone to talk to." *Sorry, Queen E., Céline, etc.*

"Will you call your maman today, please? I feel that my universe is falling apart, one piece at a time."

Stall, stall, stall. "I promise. I'll call tonight."

♡

I had the day to figure out what to do. I was so worried about what I could possibly say to Maman that I had forgotten about Luc. When I finally remembered that he had rushed off, obviously upset, I tried calling him, but he didn't answer his phone.

Mrs. Pitt met me as I was stowing my knapsack in one of the staff lockers. "Mimi, did I mention that we have a Weight Watchers group for store employees? Angela in Accounting lost thirty pounds. Think about it. Have a nice day."

Her plastic face was smooth and noncommittal. But she set off a familiar blast inside me. Yet again, somebody had noticed that I was fat. Big surprise. I *was* fat – a three-letter word, but I couldn't make myself pronounce it. Not "fat" as in "I can't fit into my jeans after Thanksgiving dinner." No. "Fat" as in "I can't fit into the movie theater seat." Forget about "beautiful" and that kind of crap. No, sweetie, *fat*. Another way to say "loser," "lazy," "disgusting," and "hopeless." If I thought that by going to Toronto I was able to leave my fat persona behind in Montréal, I was wrong. Do you have to be a Muslim to wear a *hijab*? If I wore a burkha, maybe nobody would have to see my soft overflowing tummy, my big legs, my huge butt, and the flab hanging from my arms.

I found the "Washroom for Team Members Only" (did I mention that we weren't staff, we were teammates?), and I locked myself into a cubicle. I might as well have been back at St. Mary's Academy for Girls. I scrambled to find a safe place in my mind – Las Vegas, Balmoral, anywhere but in the disinfectant-smelling bathroom – but all I could conjure up was a memory of what it felt like to be thirteen years old, eating alone, with only the salt-and-pepper shakers for company, while Macy and her retinue of admirers pointed gleefully at my full tray of food.

♡

"Hey, Mimi! Are you okay?" Someone was knocking on the door.

"Oh! Sorry!" I came out, dabbing my eyes with a square of toilet paper.

Fiona put her arm around my waist. "Remember what I told you? Pitt is a W-I-T-C-H with a *B*! She really is!"

I sniffed three times. Tante Amélie was rubbing off on me.

"When she's rude to me, you know what I do? I smile at her to show that I don't have any wrinkles around my eyes or around my mouth yet." She carefully examined her face in the washroom mirror for premature signs of aging.

I wasn't convinced that fighting cattiness with cattiness got you any more than nasty scratches, but I didn't say anything.

I began to worry in earnest about Luc when he didn't show up for work. Fiona wasn't concerned. She'd heard him come in at dawn and go right to bed. I was afraid to call him again in case I woke him up.

All day I fretted about the scene I knew I'd be

facing when I got home, so when Fiona asked if I'd like to go shopping with her, I didn't hesitate. Anything to delay the inevitable. Besides, I had never shopped as a sport and the idea was thrilling. It was not without its challenges, mind you. We went into store after store, looking for things in my size. Things that weren't scarves or hats or socks. Fiona tried on a pair of size-two pants and complained that she looked like a hippo. *Ha.* We finally found a store where the clothes were okay and they had my size. I asked Fiona, "Is this shirt flattering on me?" instead of, "Do I look fat in this?"

Fiona wasn't blind. She knew I was fat, and she was not big on tact. She looked at me critically. "Good color, nice material. It looks great on you."

After I paid with what was almost the last of my cash from home, we shared a fruit smoothie. "I usually don't like shopping," Fiona said. "I think it's such a girly, pointless thing to do, but I thought it would make you feel good."

I nodded happily and slurped up a mouthful of frozen strawberry. "You're the first person, other than my mother, that I ever went shopping with. It's fun."

"I don't know if this is any help," she continued, "but I have always hated my flat chest. All through high school, I was sure that my flat chest was everyone's major topic of conversation. *Look at Flat Fiona! She doesn't have any boobs yet.* But the thing was, they couldn't have cared less. It was all in my mind. I wasted all that energy on something that was out of my control. You're fat. It seems to me you have two choices. You can decide not to be fat anymore, or you can accept yourself. Make up your mind."

For once, I didn't go into a tailspin at the suggestion that anybody else had noticed my size. Fiona was simply stating a fact. *Was being fat in or out of my control?* It's not as if I went to Kentucky Fried Chicken every day. Even my chocolate binges couldn't account for all this weight. Maman had always told me that I had big bones, like her. Like her, all I have to do is look at a slice of chocolate cake and I gain five pounds. There's also the *filles du roi* theory. The village Maman comes from in Québec is a very old one. The first French settlers had to defend themselves against brutal winters, so the desirable women were the ones who had a big layer of fat and who were strong and resistant. They could survive pioneer life and still produce a dozen children. Maybe it's in my genes. *Or is it in the way I eat? Or the fact that I hardly ever exercised?* All the walking I was doing in Toronto was the first time in a long time that I could remember feeling the good kind of tired that comes from moving your body enough.

"You know, Mimi, if you act like you hate yourself, people will go along with you, but if you act like you deserve to be treated with respect, people will respect you."

"But what if I do genuinely hate myself?"

"Then fake it until you feel it, and, someday, you'll start believing in yourself. Lord, it's almost six o'clock. Want to come home with me and check up on Luc?"

See Luc, or face a raging Tante Amélie? Let's see. I chose Luc. I left a message on the home phone, saying not to wait dinner for me, and happily followed Fiona out of the store and down the stairs of the subway station.

The apartment she rented with Luc was in the basement of an old townhouse on Queen Street East at Broadview. It shared the block with a convenience store, a Laundromat, a funeral home, a Jamaican restaurant, and a three-storey building advertising rooms rented by the hour. The sign in the window, covered in red hearts, invited passersby in to view the seminude dancing girls.

The apartment smelled of onions and garlic, incense, and the powdery odor of books and magazines. I recognized a lot of IKEA furniture.

"I could tell you that I love Swedish modern, but that would be a lie," Fiona began. "I like this stuff because it feels good to be able to build your own furniture. It gives me a sense of empowerment" – she flexed her bicep – "and I love that."

I started to laugh, but I realized she was serious. She offered me green tea. The only place to sit was on a decrepit non-IKEA sofa covered in a faded piece of Indian cotton.

"Sorry about the state of the perch. It belonged to the previous tenant." Fiona saw me eyeing it tentatively.

The bits of wall that weren't hidden by bookshelves were covered in posters of Che Guevara, Gandhi, Bob Marley, Charlie Chaplin's *The Kid*, Popeye, a world map, and a big Campbell's soup poster. A neat pile of *Psychology Today* sat under the corner table.

I felt shy and very young. Fiona and Luc weren't much older than me, but there was something very adult about the space, a world away from my fluffy pink pillows and my pajama bag. "I see that you like Gandhi," I said.

"Yeah . . . well, Gandhi was my brother's hero. It was his poster. He passed away."

I pretended that I didn't know. "I'm sorry." The words were inadequate, but I wasn't sure what else to say.

"It's okay. He was pretty young, only twenty-one. He had his whole life ahead of him, but apparently that meant nothing to the Great Cosmos. Anyway, I shouldn't have brought it up. I don't want to talk about it right now."

Fiona was heating the water for tea when Luc opened the door.

"Hey! How are you, Mimi?" he said, and he kissed me on both cheeks. His eau de cologne was *Eternity*, from Calvin Klein (I had stowed a magazine sample in my drawer at home). I could tell that something was very wrong.

"What's going on?" asked Fiona.

"*Uh* . . . boring stuff," he said.

"Come clean, kiddo. I can tell you're upset." Fiona fake-boxed his shoulder.

"I want to show you something, and I want you to be honest with me. It doesn't matter if the truth hurts, okay?"

He opened his laptop in the living room. "Somebody we knew in Montréal sent me a message to check out Mathieu's profile on-line, complete with his picture. I want you to read it."

Luc put his laptop on the wooden coffee table.

> *Your Mother Would Love Me*
> Last updated: July 12
> Last login: July 12
> **Location** Toronto, Ontario
> **Age** 20
> **Height** 5'10"
> **Weight** 165 lbs.
> **Sex** Male
> **Ethnicity** White/European
> **Interested in** Relationship, Love
> **How "out" are you?** With my family, and at work
> **Personality** Funny, Intellectual, Introverted, Loving,
>   Romantic, Serious
> **Best attribute** Intelligence, Sense of Humor
> **Relationship status** Single
> **Politics** Lean right
> **Build** Athletic, Slim
> **Religion** Catholic
> **Languages spoken** English, French

"For the last year, I thought I was with the guy, but I guess I'm not. The last time he logged in was yesterday. What would you do if you were me?"

I am hardly what you'd call expert in the ways of the heart, unless they involve chocolate or corgis. So when it comes to love or other foreign feelings, I seek wisdom from the source: the songs of Céline Dion.

"You probably feel all by yourself right now, but love can move mountains, you know?"

He looked at me as if I had gone mad. I gave it another try.

"I mean . . . he obviously did not treat you right, even if the power of love is very strong, but you will move on and so your heart will go on too, because that's the way it is."

Stupid — could I be more stupid?

Fiona came back in the living room with a bag of cookies and wedged herself between us. "I've always known he wasn't the guy for you. How many times have I said that? He voted Conservative, for heaven's sake!"

"I know, but I love him," said Luc.

"You'll find somebody else. Look at you! You're gorgeous!"

"But I don't want anybody else. I want him. What should I do now?"

Fiona pried apart a cookie and licked the white filling. "He was a jerk — and that's not a question, by the way. That guy needs to be punished," she said.

"I don't know about punishment." Luc sounded doubtful.

"You're way too soft, Luc! I'll teach you how to stand up for yourself. Be a man!"

Luc snorted and reached into the bag for a cookie.

"Here's what you should do: create a profile under another name, write to him, and ask him questions like, 'Do you have a boyfriend? What kind of guy do you like?' Stuff like that. Then arrange to meet for coffee, so you can say, 'Good-bye, jerk' in person."

"I don't know. . . ."

"Okay. The next best revenge is to have a good time. It's not even eight o'clock. We're going out."

Chapter Twelve

J left another message for Tante Amélie. On Maman's cell phone, I left a long meandering story about the lovely dinner of tuna salad I had made and consumed in the safety of our apartment. I even threw in a hello from Mrs. Jaeger.

At last I was joining the human race, at least the segment of it that has real live friends who get together in cafés on summer nights.

"We need this on record. Say 'cheese'! Come on, Luc! Smile, Mimi." Fiona arranged us in front of her digital camera.

We looked at the little screen. "Mimi, me, and Luc! The world is ours; here we come!"

"*Mon Dieu*, I look terrible!" I said. "Well, somebody disagree with me. Please."

Luc winked at Fiona, and they led me to Fiona's bedroom. A mirror was propped on the cluttered desk. Together, they cleared a space.

"*Ta da!*" Fiona hauled a large wicker box out from under the bed and opened it with a flourish. Inside, in neat rows, was every kind of makeup, blush, and lipstick imaginable, the stuff you see in all the magazines. Fiona may

have been scornful about the phoniness of
beauty shellac, but she sure was not immune to
it herself. Rows of tubes and intriguing little
pots were stacked neatly in precise little
columns. From a desk drawer, she pulled out
what looked like a feather duster, but was a
cluster of makeup brushes.

MIMI, THE BEAUTY QUEEN

"You have beautiful eyes. Let me do something
with them," said Fiona.

"While you're working your magic with her,
Fiona, can I take a look in your closet to see what
would fit her? Tonight is *the* night, my dear
Mimi. You will be *gorgeous*!" said Luc. (Notice
how I totally forgot about Tante Amélie calling
my mother?)

"Look at you! The secret is in the eyeliner . . .
this little green bottle can turn the simplest line
into a stroke of genius! Unbelievable. Don't use
black liner. Use olive green. It's more natural.
And now, eye shadow. Luc, could you come
here, please, and tell me which one would be
best: Smoky Seductress or Bombay Beige?"

"You don't wear this stuff, Fiona. How come
you have so much of it?" It was hard to talk
because I was trying to keep my mouth from
moving while she applied the lip liner.

"I can't be bothered to put it on, but there's

something so delicious about it. Whenever I'm down, I head to the cosmetics counter. Is that crazy?"

Luc answered for me. "Yes, it's crazy. Go for the Seductress. Definitely the Seductress."

The show went on and on. Finally, I turned my face to the mirror. I actually liked what I saw. Of course, I was as fat as I had always been, but my face was genuinely different. Less pasty, and my raisin eyes looked twice as big. Luc arranged a crocheted beret on my head and wrapped a cotton scarf around my neck. I looked more *humf*, if you know what I mean (and of course you don't because I just made that word up). I looked like myself, only more in focus, as if I were on high-definition TV.

We went to a coffee bar with a pool table in the middle and comfortable leather chairs grouped around banged-up little tables. Everyone knew everyone else. Nobody flirted with me, but they all seemed cool. At first I was afraid to speak in my knobbly English, but I forgot myself as I listened to the others. For the first time in my life, I felt like a diva.

THE JIG IS UP
I was surprised that it was still quite early and that the summer night sky was still light as I caught a bus to go home. I was sifting through

the many ugly scenarios that could be unleashed once Tante Amélie found out that I had lied to her about Maman when my phone rang.

"*Chérie*, where are you?" It was Maman. Something didn't sound right. Her voice was suspiciously breezy.

"In the living room. I'm about to go to bed."

"No, you're not. You will tell me where you are, and you will do so this minute, or I will go straight to the police and have your phone records searched."

I thought of all those evenings we spent watching crime shows together. *How could I put her through this?*

"I called Mrs. Jaeger to wish her a happy birthday, and she told me that I didn't need to worry because she was checking the apartment in your absence. When I asked her, 'What absence?' she told me that Monique had mentioned to her that you'd gone to Toronto with her parents. To visit your wealthy father!"

I was toast.

"Now, I am not going to argue with you or ask you questions. I have to fly back to Montréal. You will be at the bus terminal in Montréal tomorrow at noon. Tomorrow at noon! And you had better be getting off that bus!" I had never heard her yell before, at least not like this.

"Maman, I can explain."

"There's no time. I have to make arrangements for someone to take care of Madame Tremblay. You and I will come back here by bus to pick up the car. I'm never letting you out of my sight again. Where have you been sleeping? No, don't answer that. I am so furious with you, I don't know what to say."

I knew she'd have to draw a breath sooner or later. When she finally did, I said, "I'm staying at Tante Amélie's." The words had the effect of a bucket of cold water poured over her head. I could hear her gasp and splutter.

"At Tante Amélie's? Why didn't she call me?"

"She didn't want to bother you. Because she thinks you're in the hospital dying of cancer." I probably shouldn't have said it, but I was having trouble keeping track of my lies.

The line was silent. I watched, mesmerized, as a man across the aisle industriously excavated the wax in his ear. Finally, Maman did something I would never have anticipated in a million years. She laughed. I could hear her taking big gulps of air and expelling clouds of laughter. Eventually she ran down and just hiccuped. "Give me her number. I don't have it with me. I'll call you right back."

♡

I was still on the bus when the phone finally rang again. Maman sounded exhausted. "Okay. You're staying with Amélie until I finish my contract. But only until I'm finished here. The day I drive back, she's putting you on a bus to Montréal. We'll worry about getting your things ready for university later."

I was thrilled. This was so much better than anything I could have imagined. I wouldn't have to confess to Tante Amélie about Maman's phantom cancer, and I would have time to track down my father. Besides, I could spend the summer with Luc and Fiona instead of Dr. Phil and a posse of imaginary friends. "That's great, Maman! *Merci.*"

"Don't thank me. I just don't know what else to do with you. And you're not being let off the hook. There are conditions. Amélie is not pleased, I can assure you. Not only did you dump yourself on her, but you have caused her a lot of misery. I want you to pay for your room and board, and you are to pay for your own bus ticket home. And leave Tante Amélie alone. She doesn't want any kind of worry. Try to be invisible."

"What did you say to her?" I asked, but she had hung up.

♡

Tante Amélie's house was dark. Before I went up the walkway, I tried a few calls to Salome and, from force of habit, I looked up and down the street for squashed cat bodies. I was relieved to see no signs. Once inside, I didn't turn on any lights as I made a stop at my old buddy, Mr. Fridge. I felt around for a spoon in the drainer and I scooped up a giant spoonful of butter-scotch pecan ice cream. When I finished up, I nearly jumped out of my skin. I turned to see Tante Amélie, seated in the kitchen, staring at me. All of my things were at her feet: my back-pack, a Baggie containing my soap, and my toothbrush. Her face was blank and her arms were crossed.

"How could you lie to me about your mother the way you did?"

"I can explain . . . I did it because –"

"You don't have to explain anything. You toyed with me. You laughed at me."

"But I –"

"Don't insult me by making excuses. You did a terrible thing to me and I don't deserve it."

She stood up and handed me a manila enve-lope. The cats were at her feet, savoring every second of the scene. "Here's the money to buy a bus ticket to go back to Montréal."

I started to cry. *I couldn't leave!* The thought of spending the rest of the summer in the confines of our apartment, with its stuttering air conditioner, hundreds of miles from where my father might be, made me whine like a baby. "But you told Maman I could stay!"

Tante Amélie gave me a small, pinched smile. "I lied" was all she said. She picked up one of the cats. "Good night and good-bye." She ushered me out and closed the front door behind me.

I sat on the porch with my knapsack beside me, listening to the happy sounds of a barbecue next door. The enormity of what I had done hit me. I had lied and lied and lied to myself for years. But, for the first time, I had told a lie that truly hurt somebody who didn't need to be hurt anymore. It was the worst feeling. I was used to being hurt. I never imagined it was so much worse to hurt someone else.

When Fiona opened the door in her green-and-blue pajamas, I said, "You will never believe this, but my aunt's neighbor is infested with ants, and the street had to be evacuated. Isn't it unbelievable?"

"Yes, it is." She waited for me to continue.

"Actually, my aunt threw me out."

She nodded. This was not an unfamiliar

scenario, as far as she was concerned. "Come in. I'll put sheets on the sofa."

I was a sack of guilt and blame and remorse. But that didn't stop me from sleeping dreamlessly on the greasy sofa, until I woke up to the unfamiliar morning sounds of Fiona and Luc getting ready for work.

I was still groggy when Fiona gave me a shake. "Okay, tell me about it."

So I did. I told her about coming to Toronto to find my father and staying with Tante Amélie and losing Salome. I couldn't tell her about my mother's convenient cancer attack. (What kind of monster makes up a lie like that?) I let her think that my aunt was mad because I'd lost her cat.

"That was a really lousy thing of her to do. You must feel rotten."

"I do. I'm so ashamed. My aunt hates me." I sobbed into my pillow. "I'm such a huge loser."

"I'd say that's accurate. What are you going to do about it?" Fiona sounded matter-of-fact. She had run out of patience with the *boo-hoo, poor little me* stuff.

"I don't know."

"What do you want to do?"

"I want to find out about my father and I want Tante Amélie not to hate me anymore." I snuffled into the tissue Fiona held out for me.

"Let's start with your aunt. She's real, and who knows about the sperm donor? Tell her about the cat. She can't kill you or be any madder than she already is." Fiona handed me the telephone and made herself comfortable on the floor. She wasn't going to let me weasel out of anything.

The phone rang and rang before Tante Amélie picked it up. When she did, I hardly recognized her voice. She sounded breathless. "Just a sec. I'm feeding my cat. Come here, Salome. My, you're a hungry little girl."

"Is Salome there? Tante Amélie, did the cat come home?" Tante Amélie may have been happy, but I was ecstatic. I hadn't wanted to admit to myself that I was worried for Salome, but the idea of her hungry, thirsty, and longing for home was unbearable. Besides, I wouldn't have to confess to yet another lie.

Fiona crossed her arms and peered at me as if I were an amoeba under a microscope. She mouthed the words *tell her*.

"Mimi." Tante Amélie was almost singing with relief. "I went out to get the newspaper and there she was, mewing at the door. She's hungry and she's got oil patches on her fur, but I think she's fine. Aren't you, my darling girl?" I could imagine her nuzzling Salome. "I have to go now." With that, she hung up. Not a word about throwing me out, or where I'd slept, or what I was going to do.

"You didn't tell her."

"Why should I? The cat came back."

"You're hopeless. We'll talk later. We've all got to get ready for work." Three people getting ready in a shoe box was, to say the least, a close fit. Luc cursed as he tried to keep his skipping rope from hitting the ceiling. Fiona huffed through a set of Pilates exercises and flicked her band at Luc when he made fun of her breathing. I tried to keep out of their way until it was finally my turn to shower, but by then there was no hot water. Breakfast was a hectic mishmash of granola for Luc, cold stir-fried vegetables for Fiona, and black coffee for me.

By the third night, sleeping on the sofa, with its rump-sprung cushions and old man's hair-cream smell, was only a slightly more appealing option than a park bench, but I was not about to complain. I could tell it was not a happy arrangement for anybody. Even the air in the apartment was in short supply, as the pungent odors of incense, past spaghetti dinners, and cellar mold all baked together in the summer heat.

I tried to be as helpful as possible – I washed the dishes and the tiny windows that offered a slit of sidewalk and passing feet in sandals by way of a view; I scrubbed the floor; I did the laundry for the three of us. I even invited Luc and Fiona to Pepito's Pizza for dinner. When they objected, I started to say that my maman and her phantom riches would make up the money, but Fiona said, "Shut up, Mimi," and changed the subject.

I had stalled out like an overheated radiator. Time was passing, and I was no closer to finding my father or making peace with Tante Amélie. I left message after message that I wanted to talk to her, but she never called me back. All those years of aching to find my father had seeped out of me. Even my trusty constant companions, Céline and the queen and the pageant girls, were on summer vacation. I got sidetracked by having friends for the first time in my life.

The only place I could find order was at the bookstore. I loved the cool, woody smell of the books and the muted covers. Most of the customers were pleasant enough, and sometimes they were absolutely wonderful. I recommended *Charlotte's Web* to a harried construction worker who was drilling in front of the store. He had to find a birthday present for his daughter. The next day he came in and pumped my hand. He told me that he'd started to read the book aloud to his little girl and then stayed up to finish it himself. "First time I can remember crying over a book. Thank you!"

And my English was getting stronger. It's hard to be self-conscious about having an accent in Toronto, and pretty soon, I forgot whether I was speaking in English or in French.

Best of all, I had dropped off Mrs. Pitt's radar as plans for a book signing by a famous chef consumed almost everybody in the store. Famous Chef was famous for lots of things besides his elaborate recipes: his drinking, his unreliability, and his all-round rudeness to underlings who weren't potential purchasers of his books.

Chapter Thirteen

On Friday night, the store closed early for the Coming of Famous Chef and his entourage. Mrs. Pitt was last seen screaming at the unfortunate caterer, who had provided the wrong brand of bottled water. Luc and I were not among the chosen who would fetch and carry during the evening, so after feigning an appropriate amount of disappointment, we got to go home early.

"It's a good thing we can leave because I need to talk to you," said Luc, as he waited for me to get the stuff out of my locker.

The first thought that came to mind was that Luc and Fiona wanted me out of the apartment.

"Let's go to the beach," said Luc. "I need some fresh air."

We rode the streetcar, packed in among sweaty passengers, to the eastern part of the city, but it might as well have been thousands of miles away, with its curious little shops and restaurants and the long stretch of boardwalk curving along the shoreline. Lake Ontario is as big as an ocean, and even when the city's stifling, you can catch a fishy, watery breeze. The boardwalk was busy with couples walking hand in hand, lycra-clad joggers, and mothers trying to maneuver dog leashes and strollers.

I tried to make conversation, but Luc just grunted halfhearted responses as we strolled along the boardwalk. I couldn't stand it anymore. "What's up?" I asked. "You have to tell me." I braced myself for the news that I'd be homeless. Or on the bus to Montréal. I shouldn't have worried because, in fact, what Luc had to say had nothing to do with me.

MIMI, THE CONFIDANTE

"I didn't follow Fiona's advice. I thought that if I responded to Mathieu's posting under another name, the anticipation would just about kill me. You know what I've done instead?" He drew a circle in the sand with his toe. "I printed it off and I showed it to him."

"What did he do?"

"He accused me of spying on him. Then he asked me to stop calling him. What am I going to do? I'll be all alone."

"Hey, you're not alone. Remember me? I'm here with you. When did this happen?"

"This morning. I met him at the Y before the store opened. I feel as if a big black curtain has fallen in front of me," he said dramatically. "I love him!"

I patted Luc gingerly on the back.

"I can't talk about it with Fiona. She'd say he was a jerk and to forget about him, but right now, that's not what I want to hear. She'd tell me to delete his number from my cell phone."

"Maybe you should."

"I don't want to do it alone. Do you want to help me?"

"Of course! That's what friends are for!"

He took his cell phone from his jeans' pocket and turned it on. There was a short blast of music and a WELCOME! message on the small screen.

Luc realized I was ogling it. "It's a gift from my brother François. He gave it to me for my birthday. I wish I could call him right now."

"What's stopping you?" I asked.

"I'm tired of lying to him and pretending that 'Matty' is my girlfriend. It's easier not to call."

I thought about lives we present to others, woven out of bits and pieces of the truth and hope and outright lies. It would take courage for Luc to say, *I'm gay, and there's nothing you can do to change my sexual orientation, so learn to love me the way I am.* I wondered what would have happened if I'd faced Macy and Akila and said, *Hey, girls, I'm fat. There's nothing you can do to reduce my waistline. This is me, and I'm not going to change.*

Luc waved his cell phone in the air with a grave sense of ceremony and pressed the button

CONTACTS. An alphabetical list of names scrolled down the screen until he stopped at MATHIEU. Luc took a deep breath, closed his eyes, and pressed the button DELETE until each letter of the name and each number were erased. "There. It's done. Now all I need is a brain surgeon to do mental 'delete-and-reboot' surgery on me."

We could hear seagulls screeching overhead in the cloudy sky and joggers pounding past us. I once asked Maman what she said to patients when they were feeling miserable. She said, "I don't say a thing to them. There are times when silence is more helpful than any word in the dictionary."

Luc wanted to be alone, so I took the streetcar back to the apartment on my own. It was too muggy to think about going to bed, so I walked north to Danforth Avenue, the city's Greek neighborhood. The street names were in English and in Greek, and most of the stores were painted white or blue, or a combination, like the Greek flags that fly at each street corner. I could have walked all night, all the way to Athens. Without craving a bite of chocolate. . . .

♡

I pawed under the couch for my cell phone so that it wouldn't wake Luc. "*Oui, allô?*" It was early in the morning, when speaking and thinking in English is impossible for me.

"Mimi, how are you?" Some of the frost had melted. Besides, Maman thought I was staying with a miffed Tante Amélie, and I was pretty sure that my aunt wasn't going to admit to throwing me out. "I have bad news and good news," said Maman.

"Let's start with the bad, please."

"Madame Tremblay fell and fractured her hip. She's in the hospital right now, and we don't think she'll come home again."

"That's too bad. What about the good news?"

"I'm staying for a few days to help her in the hospital, and then there's the drive home. I should be back in Montréal in a week."

Oh! Mon Dieu! Merde. Merde. Merde et re-merde. In a week? What was she thinking? What about my mission?

♡

Fiona had pushed aside my clothes to make room on the floor for her Pilates mat. "Who was that?" she said.

I told her about Madame Tremblay. "That means my mother will be back in Montréal sooner than I thought."

"Is that a problem?" I tried not to notice how

relieved she sounded at the prospect of my leaving the apartment.

"The problem is, I never found out about my dad." *And that I made my only other living relative detest me,* I could have added. "The address I have for the sperm bank is nothing but a hole in the ground, and when I tried e-mail, the message bounced back."

Fiona dragged out her laptop. "Let's try again."

A couple of clicks and it was done. She had an address.

I waited until my morning break before I phoned for an appointment. I stepped outside between two buildings to call. Though waves of heat made the street look fuzzy, I was shivering. After an unhappy false start that got me caught up in voice-mail limbo, I managed to reach a human being, who gave me an appointment for Monday morning. Two days away.

Mimi at the Sperm Bank

Finally I was sitting on a cold black-leather couch in the clinic. Although the address was different, this was where I came from. Somewhere in the confines of this office, with its floral prints from the 1970s on the wall, lay the clue to my past. I would leave here a whole person.

The coffee table was piled with women's magazines and a single copy of *Field & Stream*. I tried to make sense of an article on duck calls, but the words caromed all over the page. Finally I gave up and mentally rehearsed the speech I had written out with Fiona's help. The only other person in the waiting room was an old man. Tufts of red hair burst exuberantly from his ears. He wore a Pink Floyd T-shirt, and tattoos coiled around his left arm.

"Is this your first time here?" he said. "Nervous?"

As soon as he spoke, I realized I'd been humming. I could feel myself blushing.

All of a sudden I wanted to talk. "I come from Montréal. I'm looking for information about my sperm donor." I was so edgy, I would have confided in a fire hydrant.

"Really? I was a sperm donor myself. Years ago." He laughed and shook his head. "I must have donated a hundred times!"

I tried not to envision this.

"To be honest, I did it mostly for the money – at the time, it was $40.00 to $60.00 for each sample. I'm sure I've got kids in the double digits running around out there." He laughed until he started to cough moistly.

"Why are you here?" I asked. I wanted . . . I needed to keep talking.

"Oh, I'm here to give my written consent so the clinic can give my name to the kids who want to know who fathered them."

Mon Dieu. What if it was him? What if this oversized, overaged hippie elf was my father? Before I could take that thought any further, the receptionist called my name. I could feel my heart trying to escape my rib cage.

"Good morning, Miss Morissette." The social worker came to the door of his office to greet me. He checked the file full of notes in his hand. He was wearing a white lab coat. An old, tired man who traded in hope and disappointment. Gray hair, spotty glasses, and a sad smile. "What can I do for you?" he asked, as we closed the door and sat down facing each other.

"My mother came here over eighteen years ago, and I want to find out about my father." I could tell that I had made a mistake. "My sperm donor."

I took a last glance at the documents I'd brought from home before I showed them to him and launched into my speech. He put his glasses on his desk and rubbed his eyes.

"I was wondering if you could help me find him," I said. "I want to know about him. All I have is his ID number. I'm not quite sure what to say so that I don't come across as someone who wants to violate his privacy. Of course, I'd like to meet him – if that is an option – and of course, to have a relationship with my dad would be a bonus, but my primary goal is to learn more about his family history, looks, talents, and interests. I would also like to have some sort of medical history and an idea of how many pregnancies were conceived from this donor," I said, without taking a breath. "Brothers and sisters," I added, just to be clear.

He quirked his eyebrows at me. "Didn't anyone tell you that the information is strictly confidential? The sperm donors are guaranteed that their names will not be released."

"It's also because I don't want to have a baby with some half brother that I don't know!" I added desperately.

"I understand your concern, and I'm really sorry. There's not a lot here, but let me see what I can do. I can tell you that THEO-1 was one of the bank's most-requested donors. That's about it." He copied a few lines onto a piece of paper: "Caucasian. Red hair. Blue eyes. 5 foot 9. 140 lbs. Blood group, O positive. Interests include history." He handed it to me.

Mon Dieu! My father was slim! Perhaps there's hope for me too? He liked history! Just like me! "Wow! That's *great*! Thank you, doctor! Can you tell me his name?"

"No, sorry I can't." The reality of the few morsels he'd handed me and the finality of the words had the effect of a bulldozer. No. Something stronger: an interior Hiroshima that wiped out everything – my dreams, my hopes. I wanted . . . I needed a name to put to that red-headed Caucasian, so that I could conjure him up whenever I needed him.

"But, you must know more. It's my right to know who I am!"

"Let me remind you that your mother and the donor signed documents agreeing that the donor would remain anonymous. I had no obligation to tell you anything. If you want the law changed, go to Ottawa. Or get the donor's written consent."

I felt like stomping and yelling, *If I could contact him to get his written consent, I wouldn't need to keep trying to find him.* Instead, I tried to keep calm. "What can I do to get his written consent?"

"We can try to contact him for you, and if we are able to do so, we can ask him on your behalf."

There was a small opening in the door after all. I wrote out my address and phone number and put them on his desk. "Please, I would do anything to see him, or, at least, to talk to him."

The receptionist knocked on the door and poked his head in just long enough to say, "Your next appointment's here."

The social worker got up and held out his hand to me. I didn't want to leave the office. I wanted to put my hands around his throat and choke him. I wanted to break his glasses. I wanted to punch him in the face, to pull out each of his gray hairs, to take all the books he had arranged neatly on his shelves and throw them out the window. I wanted to wring every bit of information I could out of him. Did I do that? Of course not. Instead, I shook his hand, smiled, thanked him for his time, and left. The old tattooed man was gone too.

♡

Luc was listening to a Jacques Brel CD when I got back to the apartment.

"Hey, Mimi, what happened?"

From the bowels of the fridge, I mumbled, "He refused to give me The Name."

"*C'est dommage!*" Luc reached over my head to grab a tub of ice cream from the freezer. He took two spoons from the drawer and pulled me down onto the couch. If there's anything cozier in this world than sharing a bowl of rocky road ice cream with a friend when you've had a terrible day, I don't know what it is. The almonds and marshmallows began to weave their magic, so that by the time we were clashing spoons to get at the last lump of fudge, I was feeling better.

"That's just what you needed," said Luc.

In fact, what I needed was Maman. I wanted to feel her ample arms around me. I wanted to hear her singing quietly to herself while she ironed my school shirts. I wanted to spend a warm summer evening on the tiny patch of lawn behind our building, playing gin rummy with her and Mrs. Jaeger until it was too dark to see.

I hadn't realized that I'd started to cry until Luc handed me a tissue. I gave him a grateful smile. "I guess it's not hopeless. He could give his consent."

"And he probably will," said Luc.

Neither Luc nor I had a shift at the store that day, so we spent the afternoon watching one talk show after another on TV deal with teenagers/mothers-in-law/grannies running amok. We laughed together until our sides hurt and Fiona got home.

She listened to my tale of woe while unpacking her string bag of groceries. "Ever thought of just going on-line? It doesn't cost a thing to try."

"You're a genius, girl!" Luc turned on his laptop.

"Sit here, Mimi, I'll get a chair from the kitchen," said Fiona, as she grabbed her glasses to look on the computer screen. "Let's see what we have."

She typed three words: donor, sperm, and finding. The first website we got was about a mother and a son. There was even a photo of them. Fiona read aloud: "*Certain that donor offspring would have curiosity about their genetic origins — yet also knowing that, sadly, no public outlet exists for mutual-consent contact between people born from anonymous sperm donation — we started this organization as the logical next step to making those connections!*"

There were actually 7006 matches between 2213 half siblings and donors, but you had to be a member if you wanted to be assisted, and it cost forty dollars by credit card. I had no credit card.

"Mimi, if you really want to, I can use my credit card," Fiona said.

"Are you sure? That's what you're paid for almost three hours of work." I didn't know what to say, so I settled for a bear hug.

When Fiona managed to extricate herself from my meaty arms, she got busy with logging in. She clicked on ADD TO REGISTRY and filled out the STEP 1 form. I didn't have much information about my donor, but we had to start somewhere. Suddenly, I felt like the flower I see on YouTube: the accelerated growth of a bud into a full-blown rose.

Chapter Fourteen

No message had come by the next morning, when we were getting ready to go to work. We had been made to swear to Mrs. Pitt, on pain of death, that we would be on time. The summer reading posters and the beach book displays were going to be dismantled, and we were supposed to put up the BACK TO SCHOOL specials, though it was still July.

No message by the time we collapsed onto the sofa at the end of the day, too tired to argue about who would get to shower first to cool off. "I can't stand the suspense."

"I don't see why you're so disappointed," said Fiona. "Fathers aren't the be-all and end-all. They're just people – some good, some bad. The perfect father is a fantasy."

If she only knew how much time I had lavished over the years on my phantom father, she would think I had lost my mind. "I just want to know who I am."

"Who you are is *you*. No mystery. I know who my father is, for all the good it does me. He and my mother might as well have died when my brother died. Every bit of their energy is spent trying to track to down his heart and his corneas, as if that will bring him back. I don't count anymore. It's awful to say, but sometimes I hate my brother, even dead."

"You don't mean that. I would love to have a brother."

"You've got one. Me," Luc called from his bedroom.

"My dad had to be tough to survive. He fled the Communists and he started at rock bottom, washing dishes in a restaurant. His whole life was about giving me and my brother a chance. When my brother got into engineering, it was like they had found the Holy Grail. I was always some kind of shadow. For one thing, I'm a girl. For another, my mother's from Myanmar and her skin's dark, like mine. I moved here to get away from all the ties."

Fiona was loosening the ties, and I was looking for them.

♡

When I'd heard nothing by the end of the next day, Wednesday, I announced that I had officially given up the search. Oddly enough, giving up wasn't hard. Besides, real life was intruding. I had to get ready to go back to Montréal.

Luc had bought his textbooks for his second year of university and was leafing through a medieval text that was written mostly in Latin while I was making lists of what I needed to do before I left Toronto. The first thing was to make up with Tante Amélie. That's where I was stuck.

A comic on TV was doing a gross routine about his fat girlfriend. Luc snapped it off. "Have you seen my glasses?" he asked.

"I didn't know you wore glasses," I said.

"Only to read. I should wear them more often, but I look terrible in them."

"Stop it. You happen to look good with or without them, and besides, who cares?"

"Thanks, you're good for my self-esteem." He socked me with one of Fiona's needlepoint cushions. "Losing glasses is not a good sign. I used to be an idiot-savant when it came to remembering things like phone numbers, names, faces, but *mon Dieu*, I think I've been losing the 'savant' part lately. I'd like to believe it's not old age."

"For God's sake, you're only twenty."

"*Oui, d'accord.* I'm going to smile; look at my eyes." Luc stretched his face into a wide grin. "Did you see?"

"See what?"

"I have lines on my forehead."

"Are you serious?" I asked.

He looked genuinely upset and went into the bathroom to check his face.

Idly I logged on to Fiona's computer and checked the messages. And there it was. The end of the search. When I said I had given up, I was lying to myself.

> Dear Mimi Morissette,
>
> *After trying to contact your sperm donor, we have been told that he passed away ten years ago in a car accident. I am sorry that this may be disappointing news, but we hope it gives you peace of mind.*

I couldn't speak. I couldn't breathe. My sperm donor father was dead. I could never know him.

Chapter Fifteen

*T*hursday was my second-to-last day at work. I had been in Toronto for almost two weeks. There was a slip of paper in my employee box, where our pay slips are usually put. It was a Jenny Craig ad. I braced for the onslaught of emotions it was about to unleash on me. Let me count 'em: embarrassment that somebody else obviously noticed I was fat (I'm the one with the cosmic ability to fool myself, remember), self-loathing because I let myself eat a jumbo hot dog for lunch, anger that whoever put that wretched, innocent flyer in my box assumed that I was too dumb to think that maybe I should lose some weight.

Maybe it was the disappointment about my dad, and maybe it was the bone-weary thought of going back to my old life, and maybe it was the realization that if you let them, the bullies of the past can dog you wherever you go. Anyway, all of a sudden I was truly fed up. I was fed up of thinking about fat. I was tired of compulsively looking into every mirror I passed and compulsively hating myself every time I did. I took the flyer and tore it into a thousand little pieces to make sure that it would never fit back together.

The staff room was full. "Is everything alright, Mimi? Your eyes are so red. Would you like eyedrops?" said Mrs. Pitt. With a wave of her manicured hand, she had sent me back to Fantasyland.

Mimi, the Plus-Size Model

I am thirteen. Gym class. Change room. The girls are all here. Macy asks if I have ever thought of becoming a plus-size model. It's only a suggestion spurred by her kind heart because she wants to help me and my mom financially, she says. What she wants to do is humiliate me in front of everyone.

Patricia Tahir comes to my rescue. She stands up from the bench where she's been tying her gym shoes. "Girls, here's another suggestion. Leave Mimi alone." She towers over Macy with an I-mean-business smile.

Macy backs away. "Don't get me wrong: I just want to help. We all know how difficult it must be when you don't have a father."

When the other girls go out onto the gym floor, Patricia leans her back against my locker. "There's nothing wrong with you," she says. "I mean, there's nothing wrong with you physically or mentally. You're just overweight."

She is right. I am just fat. That's all. It's a statement like, "The sky is blue," or "Christmas is always on December 25th." She never mentions it again.

"Mimi, are you there? I'm speaking to you!" Back to Mrs. Pitt. Patricia had vanished, and I was alone in the arena.

Poor Mrs. Pitt. She had no idea that she had morphed into an army of mean teenage girls in my mind. All those years of being tormented came spilling out.

"Mrs. Pitt, did you just put this flyer in my employee box?"

Everybody was watching us.

"I'm sure that the person who left the flyer just wanted to help, that's all," she said. "We want you to be happy. You'd be happier if you were thinner. And you know, inside of every fat person, there's a skinny person struggling to get out."

"Why do you care if I'm fat?"

"Well, I care because of your health, honey, and your –"

"It's MY body! I'm not stealing any of your antioxidant age-reversing lotions. Do you think that I can exist as a human being in this century and not know about Weight Watchers or Jenny Craig or any other *Don't-want-to-look-like-a-pear-anymore* weight-loss program? Do you honestly believe that, if I had a choice, I would choose this body? How dare you tell me what I should look like, when there's so much more to me than my weight!" (I don't remember if I read that in a magazine or saw it on TV, but it certainly didn't spring from Céline Dion or the queen.)

Mrs. Pitt's mouth was wide open, as if she were waiting to be fed with a spoon. She got to her feet and marched out of the room.

"Who was that? Was that Mimi?" Luc clapped his hands. "Fighting a meany by being a meany."

Suddenly I felt ashamed of myself. "I better go and apologize. That was a lousy scene. But she made me so mad!"

♡

The apology didn't go as well as I had hoped. All Mrs. Pitt said was, "Tomorrow is your last day, isn't it?" End of discussion.

After work, I bought a ridiculously expensive ice-cream bar and sat under a big tree in Queen's Park, waiting for the long, long day to end. When my cell phone rang, I scrabbled through my knapsack for it and dripped chocolate ice cream on my white T-shirt. It was Maman, of course.

"*Allô, ma p'tite*, what happened today?" If she was communicating with Tante Amélie, she certainly didn't give any sign. And I could just imagine Amélie saying, *You know your precious little clueless daughter? I kicked her out.*

I found myself pouring out everything. About the sperm bank and the donor's being dead, and about mouthing off at work because somebody pressed the ol' Macy/Akila buttons. I felt like one of those cartoon characters who gets flattened by a steamroller. I needed her help in order to bounce back. "Tell me about Madame Tremblay," I finally said.

I wanted to hear her familiar voice wrap itself around me, though she was so far away.

"Her hip's not broken after all. She's just bruised, but she'll stay in the hospital for now. She's so sweet. She can't remember anything that happened five minutes ago, but she can remember when she was a child and everything before her wedding. Imagine having memories and then losing them. Are you feeling a bit better now, Mimi?"

I realized that I was feeling fine. Tante Amélie's office was close by and she'd probably still be there, waiting for the sky to grow dark so that she could see the stars.

Chapter Sixteen

"*T*ante Amélie, please let me in." She was in the dome room and she'd locked the door behind her.

"What are you doing here, Mimi? Why aren't you in Montréal?"

"Please let me in. I've come to apologize." I tried to sound reasonable, but my voice was rising.

A graduate student appeared in the doorway beside me. "Is everything okay, Professor Morissette?" he called.

"Just fine," she trilled, but she opened the door with a scowl that would ordinarily have sent me running. She grabbed my arm and yanked me into the dome room. "You are making a scene! Where in the world have you been staying? *Mon Dieu*, if your maman finds out, she'll kill me. I thought you were safe and sound back home!"

In that combination of relief and fury that adults unleash when you've scared them, she forgot about being mad at me. Once she had satisfied herself that I was safe, and that there was no need for Maman to know that she had set me adrift, she was angry once more. I could tell that she was revving up to blast me, so I jumped in.

"I know I did a bad thing, Tante Amélie. *Vraiment* – I really do. I don't know how I can explain it all. What I did was wrong."

"*Oui, d'accord.* It was wrong and it was hurtful. This world is confusing enough, but when you start to play with what's real, you add to the chaos. And that, *ma fille*, is unforgivable."

Unforgivable. The word shimmered in the air between us. I thought about my dead father, her dead child, and the dead time, never to be recovered, when she and Maman stopped speaking.

"Don't say that, Tante Amélie. You have to forgive me. Otherwise, what's the point? People screw up. We can't all be jumping off bridges when we do. Is this why you don't talk to Maman anymore?"

Tante Amélie picked up a crystal globe that sat on her desk and turned it slowly in her hands. "We stopped talking over something that's so silly," she began. "It had to do with an old oak chest that had been in the family since some ancestor left France with it. It used to sit in the spare room of our grandparents' farmhouse, and then it went to a cousin, and that cousin left it to your maman and me. Obviously we couldn't split it, but we both wanted it. I have no idea why.

You didn't have room for it in your apartment, and I don't like antiques. But we argued and argued. Then your mother said, 'I should have it because I want to pass it on to Mimi as a hope chest.' I had just lost Joséphine, and her words hurt me more than I can ever say. She tried to apologize and she ended up giving me the chest, but I couldn't bring myself to forgive her. I pretended that I was mad because she had forgotten about Joséphine, but that wasn't true. I was mad that Joséphine was dead. Anyway, she let me have the chest."

"Where is it? I don't think I remember seeing it."

"It's in the basement. I can't make myself look at it. Then time went on, and we forgot what we'd quarreled about, but we remembered that we were angry. You see, there's no big family secret. Just two pigheaded sisters."

There was no point in throwing more words back and forth. We wrapped our arms around each other and cried.

♡

There's no magic plot twist that involves my father claiming me as his own, marrying my mother, and moving us to Toronto so that we can be near

Amélie. And there's no escaping the tough reality of going home. My grief at leaving Luc and Fiona was as muzzy and stifled as the humid air of a Toronto July. When I opened my eyes, I realized that I had slept almost all the way to Montréal, my feet resting on my backpack. Across the aisle of the bus, a baby was happily cuddled in his father's arms, sleeping with all his might, the way that babies do. I wished I were him. The father noticed me staring.

"He'll be six months next week. He's a good boy. He sleeps through the night."

"He's lovely! What's his name?"

"Patrick, like my grandfather."

How lucky this child was to know where he came from and to know about his grandfather.

In the tiny washroom, I looked at myself in the mirror. My hair had struck strange angles all over my head. *Bien sûr*, I could have had a floor mop in place of hair and I wouldn't have cared less. I knew that the state of my hair didn't matter to Luc or to Fiona or to Tante Amélie or to Maman. Nobody else counted.

Everything seemed surreal. I took a sip of orange juice and looked out the window. The sky was cloudy, but it was not supposed to rain. So many things were not supposed to happen, but they happened anyway. I didn't find my dad in Toronto, but I found people that I will never forget. They saw beyond my waistline, and I'm so grateful for that.

I got home before Maman. The mailbox was jammed with bills and letters and flyers. I turned the key in the lock. The apartment was just as I left it, except that something inside of me had changed forever. I found myself again. . . .